DEBORAH MOGGACH

· *Smile* ·
and Other Stories

ARROW

Published in the United Kingdom in 1997 by Arrow Books

1 3 5 7 9 10 8 6 4 2

First published in the United Kingdom in 1987 by Viking
First published in paperback in 1992 by Mandarin Paperbacks

Arrow Books Limited
Random House UK Limited
20 Vauxhall Bridge Road, London SW1V 2SA

Random House Australia (Pty) Limited
20 Alfred Street, Milsons Point, Sydney
New South Wales 2061, Australia

Random House New Zealand Limited
18 Poland Road, Glenfield, Auckland 10, New Zealand

Random House South Africa (Pty) Limited
Endulini, 5a Jubilee Road, Parktown 2193, South Africa

Random House UK Limited Reg. No. 954009

A CIP catalogue record for this book
is available from the British Library

Papers used by Random House UK Limited
are natural, recyclable products made from wood grown in
sustainable forests. The manufacturing processes conform to
the environmental regulations of the country of origin

Printed and bound in Great Britain by
Cox & Wyman Ltd, Reading, Berkshire

ISBN 0 7493 1227 0

· Smile ·

I was on breakfasts when I was expecting. Through a fog of early morning-sickness I'd carry out the plates of scrambled eggs. The first time I noticed the man he pointed to the S M I L E badge, pinned to my chest, then he pulled a face.

'Cheer up,' he said. 'It might never happen.'

I thought: it *has*.

Looking back, I suppose he appeared every six weeks or so, and stayed a couple of nights. I wasn't counting, then, because I didn't know who he was. Besides, I was on the alert for somebody else, who never turned up and still hasn't, being married, and based in Huddersfield, and having forgotten about that night when he ordered a bottle of Southern Comfort with room service. At least I'm nearly sure it was him.

Deborah Moggach lives in Hampstead, North London, with a Hungarian painter and her two, almost grown-up children. She has written eleven previous novels including *Close Relations, Seesaw, Porky, Driving in the Dark* and *The Stand-In.* Her TV screenplays include *Stolen* and the prize-winning *Goggle Eyes.*

· For Mel ·

· *Contents* ·

· *Smile* ·

*W*e had to wear these SMILE badges. It was one of the rules. And they'd nailed up a sign saying SMILE, just above the kitchen door, so we wouldn't forget. It's American, the hotel. Dennis, the chief receptionist, even says to the customers 'Have a nice day', but then he's paid more than I am, so I suppose he's willing.

I was on breakfasts when I was expecting. Through a fog of early morning-sickness I'd carry out the plates of scrambled eggs. The first time I noticed the man he pointed to the SMILE badge, pinned to my chest, then he pulled a face.

'Cheer up,' he said. 'It might never happen.'

I thought: *it has.*

Looking back, I suppose he appeared every six weeks or so, and stayed a couple of nights. I wasn't counting, then, because I didn't know who he was.

Besides, I was on the alert for somebody else, who never turned up and still hasn't, being married, and based in Huddersfield, and having forgotten about that night when he ordered a bottle of Southern Comfort with room service. At least I'm nearly sure it was him.

I was still on breakfasts when I saw the man again, and my apron was getting tight. Soon I'd be bursting out of my uniform.

He said: 'You're looking bonny.'

I held out the toast basket and he took four. Munching, he nodded at my badge. 'Or are you just obedient?'

It took me a moment to realize what he meant, I was so used to wearing it.

'Oh yes, I always do what I'm told.'

He winked. 'Sounds promising.'

I gave him a pert look and flounced off. I was happy that day. The sickness had gone. I was keeping the baby; I'd never let anybody take it away from me. I'd have someone to love, who would be mine.

'You've put on weight,' he said, six weeks later. 'It suits you.'

'Thanks,' I said, smiling with my secret. 'More coffee?'

4

He held out his cup. 'And what do you call yourself?'

'Sandy.'

I looked at him. He was a handsome bloke; broad and fleshy, with a fine head of hair. He wore a tie printed with exclamation marks.

I've always gone for older men. They're bound to be married, of course. Not that it makes much difference while they're here.

When he finished his breakfast I saw him pocketing a couple of marmalade sachets. You can tell the married ones; they're nicking them for the kids.

When I got too fat they put me in the kitchens. You didn't have to wear your SMILE badge there. I was on salads. Arranging the radish roses, I day-dreamed about my baby.

I never knew it would feel like this. I felt heavy and warm and whole. The new chef kept pestering me, but he seemed like a midge – irksome but always out of sight. Nobody mattered. I walked through the steam, talking silently to my bulge. This baby meant the world to me. I suppose it came from not having much of a home myself, what with my Dad leaving, and Mum moving in and out of lodgings, and me being in and out of Care. Not that I blame her. Or him, not really.

I'd stand in the cooking smells, look at my

tummy and think: *You're all mine, I'll never leave you.*

When she was born I called her Donna. I'd sit for hours, just breathing in her scent. I was always bathing her. It was a basement flat we had then, Mum and me and Mum's current love-of-her-life Eddie, and I'd put the pram in the area-way so Donna could imbibe the sea breezes. Even in our part of Brighton, I told myself you could smell the sea.

I'd lean over to check she was still breathing. I longed for her to smile – properly, at me. In the next room Mum and Eddie would be giggling in an infantile way; they seemed the childish ones. Or else throwing things. It was always like this with Mum's blokes.

I'd gaze at my baby and tell her: *You won't miss out. You'll have me. I'll always be here.*

Behind me the window-pane rattled as Mum went out, slamming the door behind her.

I went back to work, but in the evenings, so I could look after Donna during the day and leave her with Mum when she was sleeping. They put me in the Late Night Coffee Shop. It had been refurbished in Wild West style, like a saloon, with bullet holes printed on the wallpaper and fancy names for the burgers. The wood veneer was already peeling off the counter. Donna had changed my world; nothing seemed real any more, only her.

I had a new gingham uniform, with a frilly apron and my SMILE badge. I moved around in a dream.

One night somebody said: 'Howdee, stranger.'

It was the man I used to meet at breakfast.

He put on an American accent. 'Just rolled into town, honey. Been missing you. You went away or something?'

I didn't say I'd had a baby; I liked to keep Donna separate.

He inspected the menu. 'Can you fix me a Charcoal-Broiled Rangeburger?'

It was a quiet evening so we hadn't lit the charcoal. Back in the kitchen I popped the meat into the microwave and thought how once I would have fancied him, like I fancied the bloke from Huddersfield, like I almost fancied Dennis in Reception. But I felt this new responsibility now. Why hadn't my parents felt it when I was born? Or perhaps they had, but it had worn off early.

When I brought him his meal he pointed to my badge. 'With you it comes naturally.' He shook salt over his chips. 'Honest, I'm not just saying it. You've got a beautiful smile.'

'It's added on the bill.'

7

He laughed. 'She's witty too.' He speared a gherkin. 'Somebody's a lucky bloke.'

'Somebody?'

'Go on, what's his name?'

I thought: *Donna*.

'There's nobody special,' I said.

'Don't believe it, lovely girl like you.'

I gave him my enigmatic look – practice makes perfect – and started wiping down the next table.

He said: 'You mean I'm in with a chance?'

'You're too old.'

'Ah,' he grinned. 'The cruel insolence of youth.' He munched his chips. 'You ought to try me. I'm matured in the cask.'

Later, when he finished his meal, he came up to pay. He put his hand to his heart. 'Tell me you'll be here tomorrow night. Give me something to live for.'

I took his Access card. 'I'll be here tomorrow night.'

During breakfasts he'd paid the cashier; that was why I had never seen his name.

I did now. I read it, once, on the Access card.

Finally, I got my hands to work. I pulled the paper through the machine, fumbling it once. I did it again, then I passed it to him.

'What's up?' he asked. 'Seen a ghost?'

* * *

That night Donna woke twice. For the first time since she was born I shouted at her.

'Shut up!' I shook her. 'You stupid little baby!'

Then I started to cry. I squeezed her against my nightie. She squirmed and I squeezed her harder, till her head was damp with my tears.

Even my Mum noticed. Next day at breakfast she said: 'You didn't half make a racket.' She stubbed her cigarette into her saucer. 'Got a splitting headache.'

I didn't answer. I wasn't telling that last night I'd met my father. I couldn't tell her yet. She'd probably come storming along to the hotel and lie in wait in his room.

Or maybe she'd just be indifferent. She'd just light another fag and say: *Oh him. That bastard.*

I couldn't bear that.

The day seemed to drag on for ever. Overnight, Brighton had shrunk. It seemed a small town, with my father coming round each corner, so I stayed indoors.

On the other hand Eddie had grown larger. He loafed around the flat, getting in the way. I needed to talk, but nobody was the right person. Just once I said to him, raising my voice over the afternoon racing: 'Did you know I was called Alexandra?'

9

'What?'

'My Mum and Dad called me that, but when I was twelve I changed it to Sandy.'

'Did you then?' He hadn't turned the volume down. Then he added vaguely: 'Bully for you.'

I didn't know how to face him. On the other hand, I would have died if he didn't turn up. I waited and waited. I nearly gave up hope. I had to wait until ten thirty. I felt hot in my cowgirl frills.

He came in and sat down at the table nearest my counter. I walked over with the menu, calm as calm. I didn't think I could do it.

'I thought you weren't coming,' I said.

'Me?' His eyes twinkled. 'You didn't trust me?' He took the menu. 'Oh no, Sandy, you give me a chance and you'll find out.'

'Find out what?'

'That I'm a man of my word.'

I couldn't answer that. Finally I said: 'Oh yeah?' in a drawling voice. 'Tell us another.'

'Honest to God, cross my heart.'

I looked at him, directly. His eyes were blue, like mine. And his nose was small and blunt, a familiar nose in his large, flushed face. I wanted to hide my face because it suddenly seemed so bare. He must be blind, not to recognize me. I was perspiring.

Then I thought: why should he recognize me?

He last saw me when I was four. Even my name is changed. Has he ever thought of me, all these years?

Taking his order into the kitchen, my mind was busy. I stood in front of the dead charcoal range, working out all the places I'd lived since I was four . . . Shepperton, Isleworth, Crawley . . . There was nothing to connect me to Brighton.

SMILE said the sign as I walked out.

'You travel a lot?' I asked, putting his plate in front of him.

'A conversation at last!' He split the ketchup sachet and slopped it over his chips, like blood. He nodded. 'For my sins. So what's my line of business, Sandy?'

'You're a rep.'

'How did you guess?'

'Your hands.'

He looked down with surprise and opened out his palms. There were yellowed calluses across his fingers.

'You're an observant lass. Do I dare to be flattered?' He put out his hand. 'Here. Feel them.'

I hesitated, then I touched his fingers. The skin was hard and dry. I took away my hand.

'You've always been a salesman?' I asked.

'Well . . .' He winked. 'Bit of this, bit of that.'

'Bit of what?' I wanted to know.

11

'Now that would be telling.'

'You've been all over the place?'

'It's the gypsy in my soul,' he said. 'Can't tie me down.'

There was a pause. Then I said: 'Eat up your dinner.'

He stared at me. 'What's got into you?'

'Nothing.'

There was a silence. I fiddled with my frills. Then I went back to the counter.

When he paid he said: 'I know you don't like old men but it's Help the Aged Week.'

'So?' I put on my pert face.

'You're off at half eleven?'

I nodded.

'Let me buy you a drink.' He paused. 'Go on. Say yes.'

The bar had closed. Besides, it was against the rules for me to go there. You're only allowed to smile at the customers.

But who knows where a smile might lead? It had led me here.

He had a bottle of Scotch in his room, and he ordered me a fresh orange juice from room service. When it arrived I hid in the bathroom, so nobody could see me.

His things were laid out above the basin. I inspected them all: his toothbrush (red, splayed), his toothpaste (Colgate), dental floss (so far, unused), electric shaver, aftershave (Brut, nearly finished). I wanted to take something home but that was all there was. The towels belonged to the hotel so there was no point. I wondered where he kept the marmalade sachets. But they weren't for me.

'Welcome to my abode,' he said, pulling out a chair.

I sat down. 'Where is your abode?'

'Pardon?'

'Where do you live?'

He paused. 'You don't want to hear about my boring little life.'

'Go on,' I said, giving him a flirtatious smile. 'Tell me.'

He hesitated, then he said shortly: 'Know Peterborough?'

'No.'

'Well, there.' His tone grew jaunty. Eyes twinkling, he passed me my glass. 'A fresh drink for a fresh young face. How old are you, Sandy?'

'Nineteen.'

'Nineteen.' He sighed. 'Sweet nineteen. Where have you been all my life?'

I tried to drink the orange juice; it was thick

13

with bits. There was a silence. I couldn't think what to say.

He was sitting on the bed; the room was warm and he had taken off his jacket. The hair was an illusion; he was thinning on top but he'd brushed his hair over the bald patch. Far away I heard a clock chiming.

I wasn't thirsty. I put down the glass and said: 'What do you sell?'

He climbed to his feet and went over to his suitcase, which had a Merriworld sticker on it. He snapped it open.

'Let me introduce Loopy.'

He passed me a rubbery creature dressed in a polka-dot frock. She had long, bendy arms and legs and a silly face. He fetched a pad of paper, knelt down on the floor and took her from me. Her arms ended in pencil points. Holding her, he wrote with her arms: TO SANDY WITH THE SMILE. Then he turned her upside down and said: 'Hey presto.' He started rubbing out the words with her head.

'Don't!' I pulled his hand back. I took the paper, which still had TO SANDY WITH, and put it in my apron pocket. He looked at me with surprise.

Then he put Loopy away. 'Rubber and pencils all in one. Wonder where the sharpener ought to be . . .'

'What?' I asked.

'Just my vulgar mind.'

'Where do you take these things?'

'Ramsdens, Smiths, that big shopping centre,' he said.

I knew all the places; I connected him with them. I'd bought Donna's layette at Ramsdens.

He took out a clockwork Fozzy Bear, a Snoopy purse and a magnetic colouring book.

'So you sell toys,' I said.

'It's the child in me,' he said. 'I'm just a little boy at heart.'

'Are you?'

'Happy-go-lucky, that's me.'

'Anything for a laugh?'

'No use sitting and moaning.' He poured himself another drink. 'Got to enjoy yourself.'

I gazed at the scattered toys. 'Just a game, is it?'

'Sandy, you've only got one life. You'll learn that, take it from me.' He shifted closer to my legs.

'Anything else in there?' I pointed to the suitcase.

He leaned back and took out a box. 'Recognize it?'

I shook my head.

'Ker-Plunk.'

'What?'

'You were probably still in nappies. It's a sixties

line, but we're giving it this big re-launch.' He patted the floor. 'Come on and I'll give you a game.'

He took out a plastic tube, a box of marbles and some coloured sticks. 'Come on.' He patted the floor again.

I lowered myself down on the carpet, tucking my skirt in. This damn uniform was so short.

'Look – you slot the sticks in, like this.' He pushed them into perforations in the tube, so they made a platform; then with a rattle he poured the marbles on top, so they rested on the sticks.

'Then we take it in turns to pull out a stick *without*' – he wagged his finger at me – 'without letting a marble drop through.' We sat there, crouched on the floor. 'If it does, you're a naughty girl.'

I pulled out a stick. He pulled one out. I pulled out another.

'Whoops!' he said as a marble clattered through the sticks.

'Bad luck!' he cried. 'I'm winning!'

Sometimes his marbles fell through, sometimes mine. I won.

'Can't have this,' he said. 'Got to have another game.'

He poured himself some more Scotch and settled down on the floor again, with a grunt. We collected the sticks and pushed them into the holes, then poured the marbles on top.

I didn't want to play, but then I didn't want to leave either. We pulled out the sticks; the marbles clattered down the tube.

He slapped his thigh. 'Got you!'

Outside the window the clock chimed again. Sitting there amongst the toys I thought: *Why did you never do this with me properly? At the proper time?*

'Your turn,' he said. 'Stop day-dreaming.'

I pulled out a stick. My throat felt tight and there was an ache in my chest.

'Whoops!' he cried. 'Bad luck.'

I felt a hand slide around my waist. The fingers squeezed me. He shifted himself nearer me, so our sides were touching.

'Silly game, isn't it,' he said.

I moved back, disentangling myself. 'I must go.'

'But we haven't finished.' He looked at me, his face pink from bending over the game.

I climbed to my feet. 'Mum'll be worried.'

'Come on, you're a big girl now.' He held up his hand. 'Come on, sit down.'

'No.'

He winked. 'Strict, is she?'

I shrugged. He climbed to his feet and stood beside me. We were the same height.

'What about a kiss then?'

I looked into his eyes. Then his face loomed closer. I moved my head; his lips brushed my cheek. I felt them, warm and wet. I bent down and picked up my handbag. My hands were shaking.

'Must go,' I said, my voice light.

He probably blamed my reluctance on my age. He saw me to the door, his hand resting on my hip. 'Can I see you home?'

'*No.*' I paused. 'I mean, no thanks.'

He opened the door. 'I'm leaving tomorrow, but I'll be back next month. Know what I'd love to do?'

'What?'

'Take you down to the pier. Never been to the pier. Eat ice-creams.' He squeezed my waist, and kissed my cheek. 'Know something?'

'What?' I whispered.

'You make me feel years younger.' He paused. 'Will you come?'

I nodded. 'OK,' I said.

He buttoned me into my coat, and smoothed down the collar. He stroked my hair. 'You're a lovely girl,' he murmured. 'Tell your Mum to keep you locked up. Say I said so.'

I couldn't bear to wait at the lift, so I made for the stairs. As I went he called: 'Tell her it's my fault you're late, that you're a naughty girl.' His voice grew fainter, 'Tell her I'm the one to blame.'

Six weeks took an age to pass. I had looked at

the ledger in Reception; he was booked for 15
April.

Donna was sleeping better, but for the first time
in my life I slept badly. I had such strong dreams
they woke me up. I would lie there next to her calm
face and gaze at the orange light that filtered down
from the street. I had put his piece of paper under
my pile of sweaters. That was all I had of him, so
far. I said nothing to my Mum.

On 15 April Eddie knocked on the bathroom door.

'You're planning to stay there all day?'

I was washing my hair. 'Go away!' I shouted.

At seven o'clock prompt I was on station in the
Coffee Shop. They had redecorated it on a medieval
theme and I wore a wench's costume. It pinched.

Time dragged. Eight . . . eight fourteen . . . Each
time I looked at my watch only a minute had
passed.

Nine thirty. The doors swung open. It wasn't
him. Business was slow that night; the place was
nearly empty.

Ten thirty. The last customer left.

Eleven . . .

At eleven thirty I closed up and took the cash to
Dennis in Reception.

'Not got a smile for me?'

I ignored him and went home.

When I got back Mum was watching the midnight movie. I was going to my room but she called: 'Had a flutter today.'

I nodded, but she turned.

'Don't you want to see what I've bought?' She reached down and passed me a carrier-bag. 'Put it on Lucky Boy and he won, so I went mad at Ramsdens.'

I stared at her. 'Ramsdens?'

'Go on. Look. It's for little Donna.'

I went over, opened the carrier-bag and took out a huge blue teddy bear.

'Cost a bomb,' she said, 'but what the hell.'

Next day I made inquiries at Reception. He'd checked in, they said, during the afternoon as usual. But then he had come back at six and checked out again.

Later I went to Ramsdens and asked if the Merriworld representative had visited the day before.

The girl thought for a moment, then nodded. 'That's right – Jim.' She paused to scratch her ear-lobe. 'Sunny Jim.'

'So he came?'

She pursed her lips. 'Came and went.'

'What do you mean?'

She looked at me. 'What's it to you?'

'Nothing.'

20

She shrugged. 'Dunno what got into him. Left in a hurry.'

He had seen Mum. He'd seen her buying the bloody teddy bear.

He didn't come back. Not once he knew she was in Brighton. At Ramsdens, six weeks later, there was a new rep called Terry. I checked up. Not that I had much hope; after all, he had scarpered once before.

But Donna smiled. It wasn't because of the teddy; she was too young to appreciate that, though Mum would like to believe it.

And it wasn't wind, I could tell. It was me. She smiled at me.

· *The Wrong Side* ·

*T*hey were stuck behind two French lorries, an English caravan and one of those grey corrugated Citroëns you always get stuck behind. Exhaust fumes blew around their windscreen. It was hot. They had the windows open and Bach playing, telling them about order and patience.

'Well?' Leonard asked, at the wheel. He steered out a little, so she could look.

'Yes, fine,' she started. *'No.'*

Leonard swerved back into line.

'Sorry,' she said.

Bach stopped; with a click the machine stuck out its tongue.

'Other side?' she asked, taking out the cassette.

'We've just had it.'

'Ah.' She leaned to the side, peering out. 'Try again.'

He drew out.

'Now!' she said.

He changed gear; they roared past the Citroën, the caravan and two lorries. She gradually unclenched. Years ago, on another holiday, Leonard had compared French roads to chronic catarrh: 'That slow build-up of phlegm, then a good cough and a spit and you're clear, ah but it's only temporary.'

They were driving south. They had left behind those drab, straight towns lined with telegraph poles. Now the farmhouses looked crumbly and baked. On the walls, barely visible, were faded ads for SUZE. They were passing the first fields of sunflowers; even today they lifted her heart. Their dark discs were all turned the way that she and Leonard were going. 'And half the United Kingdom,' he said, 'is going too.'

They slowed down behind a lorry heaped with tyres. Leonard leant her way.

'*Now!*' she said.

He swerved out. She felt a frisson of power, being in the passenger seat. For that split second he needed her. They shared a fear for their lives. One of the few things, it seemed, that remained for them to share.

A worse fear was that at some point he would put this into words. It was not a fact until he did so. To herself she could pretend it did not exist – to herself she could pretend anything. (Just another of the traits he found so irritating.)

26

'Where after Doué?' He changed down.

They were driving through some suburbs. DOUÉ said the sign. SA PISCINE. SES EGLISES. She scrabbled for the map, which had fallen to the floor. One holiday they had applied this criterion to England, noting the passing sights. *'Sa Tesco monumentale', 'ses car-parques multi-storeys'*, with the children mute in the rear seat. It had lasted from Mill Hill to Rugby.

'Doué . . . Doué . . .'

Anxiety made her flustered. She had folded the map wrong, of course. Red N roads to Rouen, to Travaine, ran in all directions like bloodveins.

'. . . Hang on . . .'

They had reached the centre of town. Leonard pulled up. Behind, a car hooted. He jerked forward, drove the car around the corner, and stopped. He took the map from her and shook it out, slapping it with his hand. It was ridiculous, of course, that the driver should have to do the map-reading. In Leonard's place she would be annoyed too. *Doué. Ses anglais chauds et irrités.*

'Thoars. We go to Thoars.' He kept his finger on the map, like a schoolmaster, as he passed it to her.

They drove out of Doué. Once, long ago, he had found her map confusions endearing. That holiday in England, the mad, leisured spiral of their conversation, the married inconsequence of it. *Rugby. Ses*

anglais heureux. Here in France, as they drove down
the wrong side of the road, their children having
grown up and vacated the rear seats, she thought
how subtly the right side changes to the wrong.
A process, indeed, that could take twenty-three
years of marriage and be acknowledged by neither
of them. Once upon a time her optimism had
cheered him. Once he had compared it to sap,
moving up and warming his heart. 'You call a bottle
half-empty,' she had said to him once, 'and I call it
half-full.' He shook his head. 'You, my dear, call it
three-quarters full.'

At some point his word for this charming trait
had changed. Perhaps, for fairness' sake, she should
not call it the wrong side – just the other side, like a
photograph slowly turning back into a negative, the
blacks turning to white and the whites to black. Now
he called it 'fudging' or 'fooling herself' and implied
that such anxious brightness was less fetching in
a woman of forty-three. Which increased it, of
course.

Anxiety was the taste of her days. Here, on
holiday with the gourmet Leonard, it was anxiety
that the restaurants should be neither too full, too
empty, nor too populated with the English. That
her reactions should be as he predicted, yet not
predictably dull. That, when they picnicked, the
mosquito should bite not Leonard but herself. She

never paused to consider the restaurant itself, or whether the bite hurt. She had not thought of this for years, what with Leonard and the children. Which of course had made her duller. Sometimes she felt eroded into a shell of anxious acquiescence. Hollow, and forty-three, and getting fat.

Leonard had not put on any weight. He was tall and gaunt, with the drained good looks that handsome men achieve beyond their prime. Giscard had just been defeated in the elections; Leonard had the same air of ruined distinction. In his case, though, it was not through dealing in politics but in second-hand books.

She looked at his profile. He drove efficiently. Their car was a white Rover. In England he enjoyed the deference of short-sighted motorists who mistook them for a police car; it made overtaking so easy. Here in France, of course, this did not work. They were taking the D routes to avoid, with limited success, the lorries and the English. They were travelling down to the Lot valley, the one further south than the Dordogne, to avoid the English too. Half London, he said, was in the Dordogne now, its villages full of Volvo station-wagons and children with bad manners and Rubik cubes. He reacted to British cars as if discovering a slug in the salad of France. His dread was to enter some wayside café and find it full of puce rucksacks and Birmingham accents. She had asked: 'What about them finding it full of us?'

Like herself – one day she might dare tell him – like herself the English were on the wrong side. An English car driving too fast was foolishly reckless and insensitive to rural *calme*; a French car doing the same just displayed Gallic verve. Mysteriously, French caravans were OK; he was charmed by such dedication to *la vie urbaine en plein air*. Identical English caravans, however, were just suburban. She felt some sympathy for her fellow Brits; besides, like them, her French was not as good as Leonard's.

'Now!' she said from her position of power. Leonard overtook the van. It was midday. Their white bonnet dazzled her. She kept her finger on the map and said: 'We're getting near the crease.'

'Tecreese? Where's that?'

Had he forgotten? 'The crease in the map.'

After all, it was five years since they had been to France. During holidays they had always stopped, for a celebratory drink or picnic, at the place halfway down France where the map folded, like travellers pausing at the equator. On their old Michelin map this could be, depending on the route south, just below Mirebeau, Chatellerault, or several other places she had now forgotten. After the crease one felt it was downhill all the way. Leonard had once suggested that the local *départements* should install morale-boosting placards: VOUS AVEZ PASSEZ LE FOLD in five languages.

'Ah,' he said. 'You mean it's time for lunch.'

They had already bought the picnic; the car smelt of ripening cheese and warm upholstery. She started watching out, as inevitably the road became verged with hypermarkets called *Monsieur Meuble*.

'*Now,*' she said. Then as he slowed down: 'Perhaps not.' Everyone dithered over picnic sites, she had once pointed out with spirit. Finally, miles further south than the fold, they found a canal. It was lined with poplar trees which in England depressed Leonard, reminding him of being bullied on the school rugby field, but which he liked in France, being so French. They drove over a bridge, which meant they could picnic on the other side from the road. There was nobody else about.

Leonard stopped the car. They opened the boot and unpacked the old tartan picnic rug. Leonard searched in the dashboard for the corkscrew. She laid things out. Behind them was a bush; under it she caught sight of scrumpled rubbish and old Evian bottles. She willed him not to notice them – at least not until it was time to leave. Holidays made her so tense. There was this pressure for everything to be all right. Whereas, as she knew, happiness could not be ordered on time. It swept over her at the least expected moment – not during the candlelit dinner but after it, with the striplight glaring, when they bumped into each other with some joke, and damp tea-towels. When was the last time that she and Leonard had been happy? When had she not been anxious?

They spread out the rug and sat down. Leonard had just uncorked the Corbières when a car stopped on the other side of the canal. She felt Leonard straighten beside her. A man, woman and two children climbed out and began to set up their picnic on the opposite bank.

After a pause Leonard said: 'We must move.'

'We can't. We've just got everything out.' Across the water the children called to each other in high London whines. 'Anyway, it would look rude.'

They did not move. They unwrapped the pâté and ate in silence. They were sitting in the shade of the poplar. Opposite, the English family sat in the sunlight. She did not resent them. Across the water she heard the man, quite clearly, tell the little boy not to put his fingers in the yoghurt. Munching her quiche, she envied them the simple complications of their lives. She envied that era when her own children were small; when she had actually complained about being needed too much by all three of them. Once, years ago, they had gone camping. Leonard had sunbathed on the new lilo they had bought and for one whole afternoon had walked around with a sticker on his back saying DO NOT OVER-INFLATE. In the end the children had told him, spluttering with giggles. In those days she had not been afraid of his reaction.

Across the water the children laughed, and then started squabbling. Oh, those days when the children were young, when their future lay ahead, when anything was possible. She thought of Anthea and John. Leonard found them both deeply dull, his own children.

Last year, driving home from a duty visit to John, he had said: 'One has to admire the logic. Our son's become a woman and our daughter's become a man.' There was a cruel truth in this but surely a father shouldn't say it, summing them up so neatly, like tying a parcel. Ever since then she had seen John as – well – pale and pliable. Her son was a buyer for ladies' shoes and lived in Northampton. He lived with his fiancée Cath – Leonard said that they even managed not to do this racily. She was a solid girl who wore cardigans – Crimplene Cath, Leonard called her. She sat on John's knee for hours, fiddling with his hair. The only time they showed signs of life was when she read their horoscopes from the *Daily Express*.

Anthea worked as a blacksmith in Dorking. To be exact, an assistant blacksmith which, Leonard

33

said, even denied his daughter the fleeting fame of being featured in a Sunday supplement. The forge never saw a horse. It turned out lamp brackets and toasting forks and wrought-iron gates for the sort of house Leonard called Hendon Hacienda. Anthea was large and gruff and never seemed to have a boyfriend, and said what she meant.

By late afternoon they had reached the Périgord, *région gastronomique*. The light was softer now and the countryside itself seemed sunk into repletion. Leonard, a convert to *la nouvelle cuisine*, had inspected his *Gault Millau* guide and planned stops for tonight's and tomorrow's meals. She still felt full from the picnic but she knew she would eat a heavy meal tonight, filling herself. Tomorrow they were going to the most acclaimed restaurant for hundreds of miles, *Le Beau Rivage*. Eating out used to be a shared celebration, but in recent years the pleasure had drained from it . . . him testing, her tense. The less they had to say, the more elaborately they ate.

Billboards stood beside the road. ICI! PÂTÉ DE FOIS GRAS. Giant wooden geese cast their shadow upon prefabricated huts with their wayside car parks. Poor geese, force-fed. Stuffed and stuffed, unable to escape. Leonard and she had a drink in a café, before dinner. She shuffled through the postcard stand. Amongst the slyly captioned pigs, the costumed peasants and the Dordogne rustics drinking wine out of soup bowls there was a photo of a goose, jammed by the neck in a wooden box.

She gazed at it. 'I won't eat pâté again. Darling, it's so cruel. Look they've even got a postcard of it.'

'Their unsentimentality,' he said, 'is refreshing. Look over there.' He gestured out of the window. Outside, at the crossroads, signs pointed in all directions including ABATTOIR.

'Ugh. Not before supper.'

'Oh Anna, fudging again.' He sipped his kir. 'My dear old Anna. Don't you ever *think*?'

She wanted not to think. Then she would realize how frightened she was.

The fear had been growing for months. It was worse now he had decided to take her alone on holiday, like this. Usually they shared a villa with Tim and Margot, or she accompanied him on buying trips around Britain and visited her nieces and long-lost families who once lived next door. It was more than the routine anxiety – she had grown used to that. It was fear – fear that he had brought her here to talk.

Their hotel was in the *grand confort* category. She did not want him to talk; she did not want to hear. It was a large room overlooking the back alley,

35

jammed with cars. Dustbins glinted in the evening sun. If it's another woman, she pleaded, don't you understand? I don't want to know. Haven't we even that understanding left? You have every opportunity; you stay away nights, you travel all over the place. I am soft and fat and empty. Let's stuff ourselves with food; unlike the geese, we have a choice. Two chef's hats, this hotel has in the *Gault Millau*. Let's not put anything into words. Either that there is somebody else or, perhaps worse, that there isn't. Let's go downstairs and eat that truffle thing you told me about, followed by their fishy thing for which they are so famous.

Leonard had a shower. The heavily upholstered room seemed to be waiting for an answer. She went to the window. Down there, a man lay spreadeagled on a car bonnet. It was a young man; his eyes were closed. His white apron was smeared with blood. After the first shock she realized he was just one of the chefs, snoozing in the evening sun. How wonderfully simple he looked.

'Plenty of Dutch,' she said the next day. 'No Brits, but plenty of Dutch.'

'Foreign, yes. But slow.'

It was nearly midday and they were driving along the Lot valley. The road twisted alongside the water; to one side rose thickly wooded banks topped by cliffs. A dangerous road for overtaking.

He pointed towards the roof. 'Up there lies our lunch.'

According to the map, and Leonard's description, *Le Beau Rivage* restaurant was built on the cliffs above them, overlooking the river. Last night's place had two chef's hats in black; today's lunch, however, was superior, for its two hats were red. Even Leonard, not a mean man, had admitted it was expensive. He had eaten lunch there earlier this year, when he had been down on a swift business trip – an English recluse had died and his château, with some rare first editions, was being auctioned.

Leonard swerved out.

'No!' she cried. A blind bend lay ahead. The road dipped and twisted; queues of cars crawled along it. She knew she should feel pleased, that he wanted to repeat his gastronomic treat with her. He had talked so much about this place, and now he wanted her to share it. But she felt uneasy. Leonard placed such emphasis on style. She had the feeling that he was going to fill her up with wonderful food and then say something shattering.

'Quick!' she cried. 'Now!'

He swerved out. There was a corner ahead. Her stomach shifted. The engine roared as they slipped in front of the line of cars. He turned to her; sunglasses hid his eyes, but his mouth twitched.

According to Leonard, you could tell the best restaurants by their atrocious décor. *Le Beau Rivage,* built in a small hilltop village, was set into the cliff. It had panoramic views and picture windows. Inside, a good deal of effort had been made with the furnishings: turquoise sateen chairs, lime-green paisley wallpaper, and much wrought iron – *décor rustique.* Over the violent colours hung an air of hushed good living. The restaurant was half-empty – or, as she would put it, three-quarters full. For Leonard's sake, she saw with relief just one other British family sitting far away from where they themselves were placed. Also with relief she saw that the head waiter recognized Leonard, without being over-effusive about it.

They sat next to the drop. Below, the river glistened in the sun. The road curled snake-like around its bends. The black twiddly balcony pressed against their window.

'Do you mind eating alone,' she asked. 'On your trips?'

Leonard took off his sunglasses. 'It concentrates the mind wonderfully,' he said, 'on the food.' He lifted the menu. 'One can be an object of fantasy, or at least speculation, to the other diners.'

She warmed to him. 'Last time here, did you present your left-side profile? The car one?'

'What?'

She must relax. This morning, in preparation, she had put on her nicest dress, the one with the red poppies that Leonard approved of – he always gave a detailed judgement on her clothes. By her standards it was a bold, modern print with its splashes of red. She was sitting next to the window; the sun heated her arm.

The menu made her helpless. She still felt full from breakfast. She did not say so, of course; she let Leonard order for her. An *omelet aux cêpes*, he proposed for her, followed by *le turbot clouté d'anchois à la rhubarbe*. This was what he had eaten last time, he said, back in April. He was starting with the *pâté de fois gras*. She glanced up sharply; is he telling me something? But his face had no expression.

Leonard was spreading his pâté when the fat man came in. The man was indeed immense – perspiring in his pale suit, and his face was the colour of luncheon meat. He was just being shown a table when he noticed Leonard, paused, and came over. Leonard stood up; both men smiled, shook hands and said *comment ça va?* She was introduced, though Leonard had obviously forgotten the man's name. Another smile and nod, and the fat man was seated at the next window table.

39

'Who's he?' she whispered.

'Oh, just a fellow diner,' said Leonard shortly.

'You chatted with him last time?'

He nodded, sliced a piece of pâté and spread it on his toast. She felt awkward about continuing the subject; perhaps Leonard was hushing her because of the man's proximity. But at least it would have made a subject for conversation. They ate in silence. The whole room was quiet; the murmurs and clinks were so low that she did not like to clear her throat. Even the British family, with two boys, was inaudible. Leonard had finished; a smear of pâté remained on his plate. He put down his knife. She tensed, waiting for him to speak.

'Is that nice?' He indicated her omelette.

She jerked into life, nodding. 'Delicious.' She went on eating; there seemed so many mouthfuls to be got through and yet, each time, so much remained.

What are we delaying? she thought. She had shredded her napkin; in her lap it was scattered over the poppies. That man sitting opposite, eating his *loup de mer*, he is my husband. Why does he fill me with fear? Perhaps I'm just dizzy in the sun. Perhaps we will just continue like this, making the occasional remark about the heat, and how far we will drive before evening. Perhaps there is nothing to happen.

They finished the meal. Leonard asked for the

bill and then got up to go to the lavatory. Beyond his empty chair sat the fat man, dimmed in cigarette smoke.

'*C'était bon?*' asked the man. 'It was good?'

She nodded, smiling.

'Cigarette?' he asked.

She shook her head. '*Non, merci.*' She gave him another smile.

They were sitting just too far apart for conversation, in the holy quiet of this place. She decided to wait for Leonard outside. Many people had now paid and left.

She picked up her handbag and stood up, dusting the napkin off her dress. At his table she hesitated. Having refused his cigarette, some cordiality was necessary.

'*La belle vue,*' she said, gesturing at the window.

'*Oui,* very beautiful.'

A pause. He gestured around the room. 'It is pretty, yes?'

'Oh *oui,*' she lied.

Another pause, and then she had an idea. She pointed to the fancy balcony at the window, and then to the wrought-iron brackets that held the wall-lamps.

'*Ma fille,*' she started. 'My daughter . . .' Curious how one felt compelled to explain it in English. '*Elle travaille avec les choses comme ça.*'

'*S'il vous plaît?*'

She had forgotten the word for 'blacksmith'. She pointed to the fireplace. It was hideously edged with brick, and inside it stood an ornate, empty grate, a Gallic version of the sort Anthea made.

'*Elle travaille avec . . . les trucs en feu.*' Was that right? Iron things?

He sucked on his cigarette. '*Oui madame. J'ai remarqué son intérêt.* She was liking them . . . *elle les aimait beaucoup.*'

Elle les aimait. He must mean – what was it? The subjunctive. She had done that at school, a thousand years ago. *She would like them.*

She worked it out and said eventually: '*Oui, elle les aimerait.*'

'*Le feu,*' he said. '. . . The fire, it was lighted. It was very pretty.'

She remained standing. The heat rose slowly to her face. She did not know how long it was before she spoke. He appeared to notice nothing unusual.

'*Elle était . . .* sitting . . . *assise, ici?*' she was saying. '*Ici, dans le restaurant?*'

'*Là-bas.* There, that place.' He indicated another table. 'My congratulations, madam. You have a very beautiful daughter.'

*   *   *

42

Time must have passed. She must have said something polite to him before she left. It was probably 'thank you' in English.

Now she seemed to be outside in the car park. How hot it was. The poppy dress chafed her armpits. The bright windscreens hurt her eyes.

So that's that, she thought, over and over again. So that's it. So that's that. My husband, and a girl young enough to be his daughter.

She was standing beside the Rover. She looked at its cleft, dusty tyres.

Behind her somebody was whistling.

'Know what?' said a voice.

She turned. It was the English boy from the restaurant. He was leaning against a car.

'Know what this is?' he asked again. 'Guess.'

He made snatching gestures in the air.

'What?' she asked stupidly. 'What do you want?'

'Guess,' he said patiently. 'Guess what this is.'

He snatched again, grabbing the empty air. She must be going mad.

'What is it?' she asked.

'Give up?'

'Yes.'

'It's God, trying to catch a Smartie.'

'God what?'

'God, trying, to catch, a Smartie, dum-dum.' He paused. 'He can't, you see.'

43

'Can't?'

'Can't. Because of the holes in his hands.'

It was then that her throat shrank and she knew she was going to be sick. She had managed to get inside the corridor now, pink striped walls buzzing and jarring, and now she was kneeling at the lavatory. Below her the porcelain spattered. She watched it, and the words bounced around her head. *It's not God, you stupid, stupid boy, it's Jesus.* The words bounced round in rhythm. *It's Jesus, Jesus.* All that food splashed out, all of it, the months of it, years of it. She knelt, holding the bowl in her arms.

Leonard blamed it on the *cêpes*. They were driving down the zig-zag hill, back to the main road. Her head was wedged with a cushion. He was talking about *cêpes* and *girolles* and rubbish like that. She did not bother to hear him. She felt oddly relaxed. For the first time in years she did not bother to respond.

He turned the car into the main road. Lorries thundered by in the opposite direction. They were driving towards Cahors. He said something about Cahors having a splendid bridge with turrets. She said nothing. She did not mind what he thought. She felt the car slowing down but her eyes were closed. I did not know what I feared, she thought. Not then.

'Buck up.' Leonard's voice, spoken to the car in front. 'Buck up, sonny boy.'

She opened her eyes. They were stuck behind a caravan. Leonard, Leo, my husband. Do you know what I was afraid to admit? Shall I mouth the words in the air?

That I no longer love you. That I no longer even like you. That I haven't for years.

Face up to it, you said. *Anna, you fudger. You never face the truth, my old dear, do you?*

You are cold and snobbish and faithless. Never mind about the girl; you've been faithless for so long now and she is not important.

'Anna, could you have a look?' That voice, so familiar. Tense with irritation, waiting for her to do something wrong. 'I mean, if you feel better.' He did not care if she felt better. A click, as he slotted in a cassette. Music flooded the car.

She opened her eyes and leaned to the side.

'Wait!' she said. He swerved back.

Trees pressed against the road one side; the river's railings pressed against the other. You are locked inside marriage. It has to stop you seeing those things. You don't dare face the truth.

The road twisted and turned, with its blind corners. Her stomach felt light, after its emptying. The traffic was travelling fast, but he wanted to go faster.

45

She gazed at the back of the caravan, with its GB sticker. The violins were leaping and spiralling upwards.

'Try again,' she said.

Leonard drew out. She leaned to look.

Her chest clenched. On the other side of the road, approaching fast, loomed a lorry. It was a big one; a pipe stuck up into the sky, with black smoke pouring from it.

'Now!' she shouted.

· Making Hay ·

I worked, the next day. Well, what else could I do — book one of those round-the-world cruises? Throw a party?

Mind you, I'm not ruling those out. There's months to go, they told me, and I won't be ruling anything out. But I'm telling you about that particular day, the day after I'd heard, when the sun was blazing through the windscreen, heating me up. It was a perfect June morning; you don't get many mornings like those. The sky was the colour of that bird's egg — I've forgotten what sort, but it was like a pure blue dome above me. Bloody beautiful.

I sat in the coach, waiting for my passengers. Though the door was open, there was this glassed-in silence around me. I was double-parked on Haverstock Hill; behind me, cars hooted and queued, then revved up as they drove past. What's the fuss? I thought. What's the bloody fuss?

At the delicatessen, this little Pakistani bloke was pulling out the awning, just like he must always do; just like this was a normal morning. A woman dragged her squatting dog away from a lamp-post. I thought: let him. Let the bugger relieve himself.

The trees threw dappled shadows on the pavement. I told myself I must notice this; why hadn't I had the time before? People were crossing the road as if it was important where they had to go. There was a man with a briefcase who danced back, with a hop and skip, when a car drove past. He shouted some words that echoed, far away. I watched him mouthing them.

Everything seemed sharp as crystal, that morning. Yet I felt sealed-off, as if I was in this aquarium and the whole city was coming alive outside my glass walls – people going to their offices, answering phones, painting yellow lines in the road. I suppose it was because the news was just beginning to sink in.

It's unexpected, little things you think of when you're in my position. Sitting there in the sun, I thought irritably that it had to be some little creep in a white coat, a complete stranger, who'd told me. I couldn't even remember his name. But he was half my age, and he had acne.

Then I watched some blossom float down from a tree planted outside the cinema and I thought: I don't even know the name of that tree. This made me depressed. I made a resolution to find out, and then I thought: what the hell.

I hadn't told Doriza. That's my wife. I hadn't told her all the night before; I hadn't said I'd been to the hospital. She's Hungarian, you see. Highly-strung.

Eight thirty. People were wandering towards the coach. More were coming out of Belsize Park tube station, in ones and twos. They were all women – I'd been warned about that – and some of them had pushchairs with babies in them.

'Is this the coach?' one of them asked.

'Oh no,' I said. 'It's a Morris Minor in disguise.'

'You know what I mean.' With a half-smile, she swung herself on board. Other women climbed in, unstrapping their babies. You can always tell a middle-class bunch of passengers because they get on the coach without waiting for somebody to tell them what to do.

I climbed out and went round the back to load the pushchairs into the boot. I'd already lost some weight but you wouldn't have believed it to look at me. 'All British beef,' Wally had said at the depot the week before, punching me in the ribs. Well, he didn't know, did he? Nobody did, except that bloke with the skin problem.

In the back window they'd already Sellotaped up a placard saying CND, and another one saying

WOMEN AGAINST THE BOMB. Most of them were loading their stuff themselves. They looked muscular; they were dressed like garage mechanics. I glanced wistfully at a girl passing by, wearing a floaty summer dress. But she was going to work, and disappeared into the underground.

'You've a nice day for it,' I said to one of them. I jerked my head at the blue sky. 'Not a cloud.'

She looked up, frowning. 'Not yet.'

'I heard the weather forecast. Set fair.'

'I'm not talking about the weather forecast.'

Blimey, I thought. We've got one here.

I usually like it, once I'm out on the open road. Foot down, radio playing, steaming along the fast lane at 75 m.p.h. That's the best thing about this job – the independence. They've usually all gone to sleep by this time . . . It's just you and a dreaming coachload, heads nodding, and that wide motorway with the fan blasting cool air into your face and a few dawdlers to flash at. It made a change from home, what with all the little jobs that needed doing – fixing the guttering, decorating the kitchen; well, I wouldn't be doing them now.

It made a change. Doriza likes the heating full up. She says she feels the chill in her bones; it must be her coming from Eastern Europe, and what her family went through in the war. But it makes the house so stuffy; it makes the rooms feel so small. And her leaning across the table asking me don't I like her goulash; is that why I'm not finishing it? And her needing me to hear her complaints about the neighbours; she's always squabbling with them. And why had I forgotten our wedding anniversary; did I mean I don't love her any more? Her voice, it's like the wrong tune on the piano played over and over.

It's the speed and the solitude I enjoy. But that day it didn't feel like solitude, it felt like loneliness. I told myself it was all those women, forty-five of them, and what chap wouldn't feel separate?

Someone behind me lit a cigarette. I turned round and wagged my finger at the notice, underneath the cartoons and my St Christopher, which said NO SMOKING.

'But *you* are,' she said, pointing to my smouldering fag.

'I'm different.'

'You're different because you're driving?' She shrugged – I saw her in the mirror – and grimaced at her companion. 'That's not fair.'

'You're right about that.' I drew on the cigarette. That morning I needed it.

I thought: all these years I've been a forty-a-day man; all these years I've been trying to give it up.

I looked up at the vast blue sky ahead of me.
Somebody up there had a sense of humour.

*'All things bright and beautiful, all creatures great and
small . . .'*

A few of the women were singing in high reedy
voices. I remembered the hymn from when I was
a lad; I thought, how nice they're teaching it to the
kids. But then I realized they'd altered the words.

Instead of *'The Lord God made them all'*, they were
singing *'And we destroyed them all.'*

I looked in the mirror. Through the perspex roof,
lurid orange light bathed their faces and the bowed,
sleeping heads of their children.

'Jesus Christ,' I said to myself.

It didn't sound like an oath; it sounded like a
conversation-opener. I turned up the volume on
the radio.

I'd been warned about the traffic jams but this
rally lark was even bigger than I'd expected. I'd
turned off the M4 near Newbury, and the lanes were
choked with traffic and people tramping along on
foot – men, women and children – and DIVERSION
signs. The air-conditioning had broken down and
the coach was sweltering. My shirt stuck to me, it
felt like I was wrapped in cling-film. But nobody
seemed to be complaining. Behind me the women
pressed their noses to the window and exclaimed

about the turn-out. The hedges were grey and dusty from the traffic. Beyond them, in a lush green field, black-and-white cows were munching, unconcerned. I thought: nice to be a cow.

The coach park was a large field. I sat while they filed out. I was tired; nowadays even driving tired me. Now there was a word for my exhaustion, it seemed worse. Trapped in my seat, I felt that echoing, glassed-in sensation again . . . that everything was happening a long way off, and separate. Yet crystal-sharp, as if I'd never seen a line of coaches before, or the deeper-green clumps of thistles amongst the worn grass. I realized, too, that I hadn't listened to what the women said, or stored up their daft conversation as jokes for Wally. A bunch of dungareed peace women – what a subject! He would have enjoyed that. Why hadn't I bothered to take it in? I felt panicky.

They trudged off across the field, looking purposeful. I opened the boot; the mothers took out the pushchairs. Then I leaned against the coach. Over the far side of the field there was a coffee stall. A crowd of drivers stood there; they looked as small as insects and shimmered in the heat. I knew I should go over and join them, for my own sake. I'm a sociable bloke, you see, and if I started behaving out of character I'd give myself the creeps.

I stayed, leaning against the coach, my eyes

closed. I heard the murmur of the crowd, way beyond the field, and the muffled booming of a loudspeaker. It seemed to come from another year. My passengers had all gone. I told myself I was reassured by the smell of warm metal and the diesel fumes from another coach that was just parking in front of me. Trouble was, nothing smelt familiar. Or rather, it felt only too familiar but it was out of reach. It was like the first day at school, when you're closed off in a classroom and you hear the familiar noises in the street outside but you can't get at them. Like that, but worse.

I was thinking about Doriza, and how I'd have to tell her. Sooner or later, I'd have to. 'Why don't you finish it up?' she'd been asking me recently. 'You don't like my cooking?' Our kitchen seemed so cramped with her in it, fussing me. I suppose most marriages aren't as happy as people hoped, if we're being truthful about it. (I was telling myself the truth that day, for the first time. You would too, in my position. The truth, it rears up and stares you in the face.) Fifteen years ago, when we first met, we had this fiery relationship. I'd met her at Paddington Station and she'd been what they'd call voluptuous. Wally would say big tits but it was more than that, she seemed soft and scented and foreign. Mysterious. But mystery's the first thing to wear off, isn't it?

If we'd had children it would have been different. She's always seemed so dissatisfied. She's always asking me if I love her. If I get up to go to the toilet she asks me where I'm going. If I'm reading the paper she asks me to read it out loud. Sometimes I feel my head's going to burst. Don't get me wrong, I'm still fond of her. We're probably no worse than most people. Maybe if we'd had kids we'd have had more in common.

Dolly (I call her that), *Dolly, I've got something to tell you . . . Know how I've been feeling not quite the ticket? . . .*

A skeleton climbed out of the coach opposite me. Well, it was somebody wearing a skeleton suit. He or she loped off down the field, amongst the crowds of people.

I closed my eyes; the sun beat down on my face. I imagined Doriza smothering me in her arms – she's a big woman – and soaking me with her tears. I imagined us having to be loving to each other, all the time. After this, we'd never be able to lose our tempers. I imagined the house hushed, and hotter, and closing in around me. I thought of Wally and Dave, my partners, shutting up when I came into the depot office . . . shuffling their feet and stopping their jokes.

*   *   *

I went to lock up the coach. There was somebody still sitting in it.

'Hello,' I said. 'We've arrived.'

'I know. I felt queer. Ill.' She paused. 'It must be the sun.' She was sitting in an aisle seat, near the front. 'I felt awful on the motorway,' she said. 'I thought I was going to be sick.'

'On my new velour? You wouldn't dare.'

She looked pale, but then she was one of those redheads, with that white skin. Nearer to, I could see she was covered with freckles. Her hair was bushy; in the orange light it was like a halo around her face.

'Yes, you do look peaky,' I said.

'Great. Thanks.'

'Sorry.'

'I'm not marching. I'd probably faint and let everybody down. I'll just stay in the coach.'

She didn't. She climbed through a fence with me; we walked across two fields until we came to a little triangular meadow where they'd been cutting hay. Woods closed it in on two sides; there were bales stacked up all over the place. We sat against a pile of them. Above us there were larks singing – well, I think they were larks – and the occasional clackety-clack of a police helicopter.

She was young enough to be my daughter. You

should've seen her hands; they were so small, with faint bluish veins at the wrists.

'I feel better,' she said. 'I'm a bit anaemic, that's why.'

We sat there for quite a while, in silence. She seemed to think it was perfectly natural, just to sit there with her coach driver. I didn't mind. I didn't mind anything, that day. It all seemed unlikely. I'm not in the habit of sitting in fields.

She closed her eyes. Most women feel they have to talk all the time, but she didn't seem afraid of the gaps.

For the first time since I'd heard the news I felt peaceful. I suppose it was the countryside, and the fact that she didn't ask any questions. She was a stranger, and I didn't have to tell her anything. Just because of that, I felt she was the only person I could tell.

Before I could speak, she opened her rucksack. 'Want a sandwich?'

'I've got some in the coach.'

'Have one of mine.' She passed me a doorstep of brown bread, packed with cheese and pickle and cucumber, and started wolfing down hers. For such a frail girl she had quite an appetite.

She paused, with crumbs on her lips. 'You don't want any more?'

I gave her back the other half. 'You finish it.'

'Why?'

'I'm not that hungry.'

'You'll waste away.'

I looked at her sharply.

'Only joking,' she said, prodding my solid chest. That decided me not to tell her.

She ate in silence, tearing at the crust. It did me good to watch her. Finally she swallowed the last mouthful.

'Got any kids?' she asked.

I shook my head. 'Nope.'

'All those kids in the coach, they made me feel so sad.'

'Why?'

She paused. 'Actually, I suppose they just thought it was a day out in the country.' She was silent, staring at her toes. She'd kicked off her plimsolls.

'I'd have liked to have kids,' I said.

She swung round and stared at me. 'Would you?'

'Yes,' I said, realizing just how much. 'Why not?'

She gestured at the field, then up at the blue sky. 'What, bring them into this world?'

'Looks beautiful to me.'

She made an impatient sound, and turned away. What was the matter with her? A young girl like her, who'd eaten her sandwiches with such relish, greedy as a child, she shouldn't be talking like this. I looked at her horrible baggy khaki trousers, and her T-shirt the colour of mud. A lovely-looking girl like her ought to be wearing something bright . . . a mini dress. Something pretty, that would do her justice. I imagined her legs, under the trousers. Her ankles were as slender as a bird's.

She turned back. 'What's your name?'

'Frank.'

'Listen, Frank, don't you understand?' She stopped and sighed. 'Oh, I wish I'd gone on the march.'

'What's your name?'

'Tessa.'

'Tessa . . .' I mulled over the name, fitting it to her. Then I grinned. 'I know why you didn't. So you could sit here with me.'

She frowned. 'What?'

'Only joking. Don't mind me.' I paused. 'I mean it – you've made me feel a lot better.'

'I couldn't have.'

'No, honest.'

She flung back her head. 'It wouldn't have done any good anyway.'

'But I just said – it has.'

'I mean going on the march. Just a bunch of people.'

'Well, you've done *me* good. One person.'

She squinted at me, the sun in her face. 'But

what the hell are you and me? What can either
of us do?'

She had a small, flat, hard voice. I wondered how
she'd sound when she was laughing. She ought to
be laughing – a beautiful girl like her, on a beautiful
day like this. And she shouldn't be wearing those
depressing clothes.

I wondered how her hair would feel – soft or wiry.
I imagined picking wild flowers and putting them
into her hair. She'd probably slap my face. Anyway,
the hay was cut and there was only stubble left.

Beyond the woods, a helicopter clattered. Suddenly she turned and grabbed me. Before I could
do anything, she pulled me towards her.

'Frank, I'm frightened.'

'It's only a chopper.'

She pressed her face into my chest. She repeated
in a low voice: 'I'm frightened.'

I put my arms around her. She felt even more
frail than she looked. I held her against me, feeling her sharp shoulder-blades and the knobs of
her backbone. I pressed her bushy hair against
my chest, bending my head and smelling her.
She smelt of soap, and warm skin. She smelt
young.

I said: 'Not as frightened as me, love.'

We clutched each other, rocking. The hay bales
bumped our sides. Far away I heard the hooting of

cars in the endless traffic jams, and the sound of a tannoy.

Then she disentangled herself, and in one violent movement she pulled her T-shirt over her head. She bent over to unbutton her trousers. For a mad moment I thought she was going to sunbathe. Then she swung round, tossing back her mass of hair.

'Come on.' Her voice was flat.

'But –'

'You afraid? Who cares?' She gestured at the woods. 'Life's too short.'

'But –' I started again, and stopped. To be honest, this sort of thing doesn't happen to me that often. Like, never. But wasn't she going to smile or something?

She moved her face towards mine. I looked at her white, freckled skin and her dry lips. She searched my face, seriously. Then we kissed. I hadn't kissed anybody for a long time. She started unbuttoning my shirt and I tried to help her, with my clumsy hands, but before we'd finished she pulled me down on top of her, and wrapped her bare legs around me, holding me fast.

Greedily she wanted more. She gripped me; there was something impersonal and determined about the way she did it. She kissed me, her tongue pushing into my mouth; she ran her lips down my neck, but when I drew back to speak she twisted her head away and just pulled me towards her again. Once she bit my shoulder, hard.

At last she lay back, panting. Her skin was shiny with sweat. She was very thin; her breasts were so small they were barely there – just soft, pale nipples and a freckled chest. I wanted to hold her in my arms, but she was lying absolutely still, gazing up at the sky. She hadn't smiled, once.

There was a silence. Then she said: 'Make hay while the sun shines.'

'What about "Make love while the sun shines"?' I said, trying to be friendly.

'Love?' She turned, and squinted at me. Then she said, in that flat voice: 'I'd call it despair.'

I parked the coach outside Belsize Park tube. There was this golden evening light across the parade of shops. Above the delicatessen the awning was still out; it seemed unbelievable that the shops had been open all this time, and that it had only been one day.

I missed her. By the time I'd opened the boot, she'd got out of the coach. When I straightened up and turned, I saw her disappearing into the tube; she was hitching the rucksack over her back.

I drove home from the depot and sat in the car outside our front gate. I knew what I was going to say; the words had been rolling round my head since the night before.

Dolly, I've got something to tell you. I'm not just off-colour . . . (How could I put it?) *As a matter of fact, I've got leukaemia.*

I've got leukaemia and I'll spend the rest of my days, short though they are, here in this overheated house with you, pretending we've always been happy. I'll have to behave like a saint because nobody, you or Wally or anyone, will let me behave like a jerk.

Life's too short. That's what she'd said.

Doriza was in the lounge, eating marzipan fancies. I paused at the door, and opened my mouth.

Then the words came out.

'Dolly, I've got something to tell you.' I walked in and stopped in front of the gas fire. The words were different than I'd meant. 'Today I met this girl, this bird . . .'

Suddenly I felt airy inside, and lighter. The words came out in a rush.

'See, we went into this hayfield . . .'

Dolly stopped munching and stared at me.

I watched her expression change.

· *Empire Building* ·

*I*t didn't look much when he took it over, the Empire Stores, but a man with business instinct could see the potential. The previous owners had been fined by the Health Authority and finally gone bust. Hamid, however, had standards. His wife told people this too, with a small shake of her head as if she were being philosophical about it.

The neighbourhood was a transient, shabby one, with terraces of bedsits and Irish lodging houses. The parade of shops, Hamid calculated, was far enough from the Holloway Road for people to rely upon it for their local needs, which he had all intention of supplying. The shops were as follows: a wholesale dressmaking business with a curtained window behind which the sewing machines hummed – those Greek ladies knew the meaning of hard work; a dentist's surgery with frosted glass; a greengrocer's that had ageing fruit and

early closing on Thursdays – now how can anyone prosper with early closing; then the Empire
Stores, and next door to it a newsagent's run
by an indolent Hindu and his wife. Hamid put
a notice UNDER NEW MANAGEMENT in the window of the Empire Stores and re-stocked the mer-
chandise – liquor behind the cash desk, where
he sat in control, and groceries along the aisles.
His aims were not modest, but his beginnings
were.

His own wife and children were installed in
a flat in Wood Green, three miles away, where
the air was fresher and the neighbourhood more
salubrious. The streets around the Empire Stores
were not respectable; you need only have taken a
look at the cards fixed to the newsagent's window
– even a family man like Hamid knew the meaning of those kind of French Lessons. Business is
business, however, and it is a wise shop keeper
who is prepared to adapt. Or, as his father was
fond of saying: to those who are flexible comes
strength.

The local blacks were big West Indians who
drove up in loudly tuned cars and who suddenly
filled the shop. They bought party packs of beer in
the evenings and left a musky male scent behind
them. One of the first things Hamid did was to
extend his opening hours until 9 p.m. Then there

were the single young ladies who bought Whiskas and yoghurt and disappeared into the sodium-lit streets. How solitary was the life of these young English women with no family to care for them; no wonder they fell into evil ways. Hamid installed a second cold shelf and stocked it with pizzas, two ranges of yoghurts and individual fruit-juice cartons for these bedsit dwellers and their twilit lives. Such items moved fast.

Sitting at the till, its numbers bleeping, Hamid thought of the dinner being prepared for him at home – the hiss of the spices as they hit the pan, the buttery taste of the paratha he would soon be eating. He thought of his son Arif, his neat, shiny head bent over his homework, the TV turned right down. He thought of his own tartan slippers beside the radiator. Passing them a carrier-bag, he gazed with perplexity at these lost, pasty-faced English girls.

His main income, however, came from the drunks. It was for them that within the first three months he had doubled the bottle shelf-space and increased his range of cans. Business was brisk in Triple Strength Export Lager. These men, their complexions inflamed by alcohol, shambled in at all hours, muttering at the floor, murmuring at the tins of peas. They raised their ruined faces. Hamid avoided their eyes; he took their soiled bank notes or the coins they counted out, shakily, and fixed his gaze above their heads. Flesh upon flesh, sometimes their fingers touched his, but he was too well-mannered to flinch. Sometimes they tried to engage him in conversation.

It was bemusing. Not only did they poison themselves with drink, rotting their souls and their bodies, but they had no shame. They leaned against the dentist's frosted glass, lifting the bottle to their lips in full public view. They stood huddled together in the exit of the snooker hall, further up the road, where warm air breathed from the grilles. Sometimes he could hear the smash of glass. Lone men stood in the middle of the road, shouting oaths into the air.

Business is business. Sometimes he raised his eyebrows at Khalid, his nephew, who helped him in the shop, but he never offended his wife by describing to her this flotsam and jetsam. One night she said: 'You never talk to me.'

It was the next week that a man stumbled in and steadied himself against the counter. He asked for a bottle of cider and then he said: 'You'll put it on the slate?'

'I beg your pardon?' Hamid raised his eyes from his newspaper.

'I'll pay tomorrow.'

'I'm sorry,' Hamid said. 'It is not shop policy.'

The man started shouting. 'You fucking wog!' he yelled, his voice rising.

Hamid lowered his gaze back to the dancing Urdu script. He turned the page.

'Get back to the fucking jungle, fucking wog land!' the voice slurred – 'where you belong!'

Khalid appeared from the stock-room and stood there. Hamid kept his eye on the page. He read that there was a riot in Lahore, where an opposition leader had been arrested, and that ghee was up Rs 2 per seer.

'Fucking monkeys!'

Khalid put down the crate of Schweppes and escorted the man to the door. The next day Hamid wrote a notice and Sellotaped it to the counter.

He sat there, as grave as always, in his herringbone tweed jacket. He held himself straight as the men shambled in, those long-lost rulers of a long-lost Empire, eyeing the bottles behind him. He had written the notice in large red letters, using Arif's school Pentel: PLEASE DO NOT ASK FOR CREDIT AS A REFUSAL OFTEN OFFENDS.

That was in the late seventies. War was being waged in the Middle East; a man had walked on the moon; Prince Charles had still not found a wife. Meanwhile Hamid filled out his VAT receipts, and in view

73

of increased turnover negotiated further discount terms with McEwans, manufacturers of lager.

In 1980 the old couple who ran the greengrocer's retired and Hamid bought the shop, freehold, and extended his own premises, knocking through the dividing wall and removing the sign H. LAWSON FRUITERER AND GREENGROCER.

Apart from 'good morning', the first and last conversation he ever held with the old man was on completion day, when they finalized the transaction in the lawyer's office down the road.

'Times change,' said the old man, Mr Lawson. The clock whirred, clicked and chimed. He sighed. 'Been here thirty years.'

They signed the document and shook hands.

'Harold,' said Hamid, reading the signature. 'So that's your name.'

'You know, I was in your part of the world.'

'My part?' asked Hamid.

'India.'

'Ah.'

'In the army. Stationed near Mysore. Know it?'

Hamid shook his head. 'My family comes from Pakistan.'

They stood up. 'Funny old world, isn't it,' said the old man.

Hamid agreed, politely. The lawyer opened the door for them.

74

'How about a quickie,' said the old man.

'I beg your pardon?'

'Little celebration.'

Hamid paused. 'I don't drink.'

They reached the head of the stairs. 'No,' said the old man. 'No, I suppose you don't. Against your religion, eh?'

Hamid nodded. 'You first, please,' he said, indicating the stairs.

'No, you.'

Hamid went first. They emerged into the sunlight. It was a beautiful day in April. Petals lay strewn in the gutter.

'If I'd been blessed with a son, maybe this wouldn't be happening,' said the old man. 'But that's life.'

Hamid nodded.

'You've got a son?'

'Yes,' said Hamid. 'A fine chap.'

'Expect he'll be coming in with you, in due course.'

Hamid murmured something politely; he didn't want to offend the old man. Arif, running a shop? He had greater things in mind for his son.

Hamid had a new, larger sign fitted to cover the new, double shop-front and this time had it constructed in neon-illuminated script: THE EMPIRE STORES.

He extended both his liquor and grocery range to cover the extra volume of retail space, adding a chicken rotisserie for take-outs, a microwave for samosas and a large range of fruit and vegetables – all of a greatly improved quality to those of H. Lawson. The old man had left the place like a junk heap; it took seven skips to clear the rubbish out of the upper floor and the backyard. One morning Hamid was out in the street, inspecting a heaped skip, when one of his customers stopped. She was an old woman; she pointed at the skip with her umbrella.

'See that?' she said. 'The wheels? Used to have a pony and cart, Harry did. For the deliveries.'

'Did he really?' Hamid glanced up the street. He was waiting for the builders who were late again. Unreliable.

'Knew us all by name.' She sighed and wiped her nose. 'No . . .' She shook her head. 'Service is not what it was.'

'No,' agreed Hamid, looking at his watch and thinking of his builders. 'It certainly isn't.'

Hamid, who always bought British, traded in his old Cortina and bought a brand-new Rover, with beige upholstery and stereo-player. He transferred Arif to a private school, its sign painted in Gothic script, where they sang hymns and wore blazers.

On Parents' Day the panelled halls smelt of polish; Hamid gazed at the cabinets of silver cups. His wife wore her best silk sari; her bangles tinkled as she smoothed Arif's hair.

The conversion of the upper floors, above the old fruit shop, was completed at last and Hamid stood on the other side of the street with Khalid and his two new assistants. He looked at the sunlight glinting in the windows; he looked at the dazzling white paint and the sign glowing below it: THE EMPIRE STORES. His heart swelled. The others chattered, but he could not speak.

That night Arif stood, his eyes closed and his face pinched with concentration, and recited:

> *'Earth has not anything to show more fair:*
> *Dull would he be of soul who could pass by*
> *A sight so touching in its majesty:*
> *This City now doth, like a garment, wear*
> *The beauty of the morning; silent, bare,*
> *Ships, towers, domes, theatres, and temples lie*
> *Open unto the fields, and to the sky;'*

His eyes opened. 'Know who it's by?'

Hamid shook his head. 'You tell me, son.'

'William Wordsworth. We're learning it at school.'

For the second time that day, Hamid's heart swelled. He put his arms around his son, the boy

77

for whom everything was possible. He pressed his face against his son's cheek.

1981. Ronald Reagan became President of the USA. In May the Pope was shot and wounded. In Brixton there were riots; Toxteth too. In July Prince Charles married his Lady Di.

Khalid, too, was married by now and installed in the first-floor flat above the shop. National holidays were always good, business-wise; by now the Empire Stores was open seven days a week and during that summer's day, as people queued at the till, Hamid kept half an eye on his portable TV set. A pale blur, as Lady Di passed in her dress; a peal of bells. As Hamid reached for the bottles of whiskey, the commentator's voice quickened with pride and awe, and Hamid's heart beat faster. 'Isn't she a picture,' said his customers, pausing at the screen. Hamid agreed that, yes, she was the most radiant of brides. Flags waved, flicking to and fro, and the crowd roared. Our Princess, his and theirs . . . Hamid smiled and gave a small boy a Toblerone.

That night his wife said: 'You should have seen it in colour.'

Hamid pulled off his shoes. 'You've put it on the video-tape?'

She nodded and turned away, picking up the

scattered jigsaw in front of the TV, where his daughters had been sitting.

'We can watch it later,' he said.

'When?' Her voice was sharp. He looked up in surprise. 'It's not the same,' she said, closing the box.

That night a bottle was thrown up through the window of Khalid's flat. It shattered the glass; Khalid's bride cowered in the corner.

The next day, while the Royal couple – oh how happy they looked – departed on their honeymoon, Hamid inspected the damage. He gazed down into the street, through the wicked edges of glass. They were intruders, those people entering the Empire Stores. Yesterday's glory had vanished. Hamid sat down heavily, on the settee.

'How could they do this to us?' he asked. 'What have we done to deserve it?'

Khalid, who was an easy-going chap, said: 'Forget it. They were just celebrating.' He lowered his voice, so his bride couldn't hear. 'They were one over the eight.'

'What?'

'Drunk.'

Drunk on the drink he had sold to them. Yesterday they had had record takings.

He closed up the shop that night and walked to

his car. On the pavement lay a man, asleep, his face bleeding. Cans lay around him. Hamid remembered how once, years ago, he had called an ambulance when he had found a person in this state.

Now he just made a detour on the other side of the pavement.

That autumn he installed closed-circuit surveillance in the shop. He now had three assistants and an expanded range of take-away food. Children from neglectful homes came in with shopping bags; they had keys around their necks, and runny noses. They bought bars of Kit Kat and crisps and hot pasties. These mothers did not look after their youngsters; they sent them into the streets to consume junk food.

The dressmaker's was taken over by a massage and sauna establishment, which installed black glass and a Georgian door. All about lay the ruined and the dispossessed. This was their country but these people had no homes. New, loitering men replaced the old. Strange faces appeared for a week, a month, and then after a while he would realize they had vanished. To where? His neon sign shone out over the drab street. Inside the shop lay the solace of food, and order.

That year his turnover doubled. He fitted out an office in the store-room and managed his growing empire from there, drinking tea from his Charles and Di commemoration mug. He had now converted four flats above the shop, and the lease of the newsagent's shop next door was coming up shortly; he had his eye on that.

In an attempt to brighten the neighbourhood, the council had planted young trees along the pavement. Their leaves were turning red and falling to the ground. Opposite, the sunset flamed above the chimney-pots. As he said his evening prayers on the mat behind his desk, he felt both humbled and grateful.

That evening he looked into his girls' bedroom. They were two sleeping heads. Arif was in the lounge, bent over his computer game. Hamid ruffled his hair; Arif smoothed it down again.

'And have you a hello for your father?'

Arif pressed a button. '570,' he said. '680.'

Later, when Arif was asleep and Hamid had eaten, he said to his wife: 'They teach them no manners at that expensive school?'

She turned, 'You think you can buy manners with money?'

He looked sharply at her. She was putting the crockery away in the cabinet.

'What are you trying to say?' he asked.

'Manners are taught by example. At home.'

'And don't I set a good example?'

'When you're here.' She sighed, and shut the cabinet. 'I think he is suffering from neglect.'

'You say that about my son?'

Neglect? Hamid thought of the boys with faces like old men's, and keys around their necks. Pale boys buying junk food.

'It's his age,' said Hamid loudly, surprising himself. 'He's fourteen now. A difficult age.'

'If you say so.'

She sighed again and reached up for something on the top of the cabinet. It was a box of Milk Tray. How plump she was becoming; her kurta was strained tight over her belly.

'Come to the shop,' he said, 'and there I'll show you the meaning of neglect.'

She sat down, shaking her head in that philosophical way. More and more she irked him by doing this. She examined a chocolate and popped it into her mouth. He looked at her and the word rose up: junk food.

He ignored this. Instead he asked: 'Doesn't Arif understand? I'm working for him. For all the family.' He ran his fingers through his hair. 'For the future.' His voice rose higher. She glanced warningly towards the bedrooms. 'I'm working so that he need never work in a shop! You understand me, woman? Can't you understand?'

She said nothing, though she tilted her head. He

thought she was assenting, but then he saw she was just choosing another chocolate.

Hindus are lazy. History has proved that point. Their religion is a dissipated one; their life-style one of self-indulgence, of the inaction that comes from fatalism. Take Mr Gupta's attitude, for example, to the expiry of his lease. He smiled and raised his hands: the new price was too high; he had this trouble with his stomach; he had been robbed three times in the past year. What will be, will be . . .

Hamid would have suggested that Mr Gupta invest in vandal-proof shuttering, as he himself had done. But he could always have that fitted when he took over the lease, which he did just as the trees outside frothed into blossom, in celebration.

Islam is a progressive faith. He progressed, removing Mr Gupta's sign and installing THE EMPIRE NEWSAGENTS over the door. He now had one double shop and one single; his properties dominated the parade of shops. Indeed, that week several of his customers joked that he'd soon be taking over the street. Hamid smiled modestly.

The state of that shop! The squalor and the unexploited sales area! The possibilities! It was a dusty little con-tob newsagent's when Hamid took it over, but after a complete refitment he had doubled the shelf space and the stock, and introduced fast-profit items including a rental Slush-Puppy dispenser in six flavours – a favourite with the local latch-key children.

Dirty magazines, he was not surprised to discover, had a brisk sale in this neighbourhood and he increased the stock from seven titles to fourteen. *Knave* and *Mayfair*, bulging flesh . . . he kept his eyes from this nude shamelessness. He placed such journals on the top shelf. Boys little older than Arif came in to giggle and point; they stood in a row on his display bases. These boys, he thought, they are somebody's son; does nobody cherish and protect them?

It was during the first month of business that Hamid opened the local newspaper and read: 'We are sad to announce the death of Mr Harold Lawson, universally known as Harry to his customers and many friends. For thirty years he was a well-loved sight on the local scene, with the fondly remembered Betty, his pony . . .'

Hamid read on. It concluded: 'A modest man, he seldom mentioned his distinguished army record, serving with the King's Rifles in India and being awarded a DSO for his bravery during the Independence Riots. He leaves a widow, Ivy, and will be sorely missed. It can truly be said that "they broke the mould when they made Harry".'

Outside the petals had blown into the gutter, just

as they had lain the day Hamid had accompanied
the old man into the street two years earlier. It was
the slack mid-morning period and Hamid stood in
the sunshine, watching the clouds move beyond the
TV aerials. For a moment he thought of the earth
rolling, and history turning. He himself was fond of
poetry, despite his lack of education. What was it
Arif used to recite? 'Deign on the passing world to
turn thine eyes,/And pause awhile from letters to
be wise.'

That evening he asked Arif who was the English
poet who had written those words. William Shakespeare?

'Dunno.'

Hamid placed his hand on his son's shoulder. 'No,
that's "All the world's a stage",' he said. Arif's bones
were surprisingly frail. He sat with his eyes on the
TV screen where first a house, then a car, burst
into flames.

Hamid kept his son's exercise books on a special
shelf. He searched through and found the quotation,
written in the round, careful writing Arif still had a
year or so ago.

'Ah. Samuel Johnson.'

Hamid raised his voice; on the TV a siren
wailed.

'Remember?'

He looked at the title: *The Vanity of Human Wishes*.

Arif said: 'You're blocking my view.'

1983. Renewed fighting in the Lebanon, and the film *Gandhi* won eight Oscars. There were fires and floods in Australia and peace people made a human chain around Greenham Common. The future King of England was toddling now, so was Khalid's first-born son in the flat above the Empire Stores. Property was moving again, as the worst of the recession was said to be over, and Hamid converted the upper floors above the newsagent's shop and sold the flats on long leases.

With the profits, and another bank loan, that summer he bought a large detached house for his family, a real family home in that sought-after suburb, Potters Bar.

'I have worked twenty years for this moment,' he said, standing in the lounge. There were fitted carpets throughout. There was even a bar in panelled walnut, built by the previous owners who had amassed large debts both by drinking and gambling, hence the sale of this house. He pictured his children sitting around the bar, drinking blameless Pepsi.

'This is the proudest moment of my life,' he repeated, his words loud in the empty room. Through its french windows there was a view of the garden, a series of low terraces separated by balustrades. Two small figures in orange anoraks stood on the lawn: his daughters.

Arif, however, was nowhere to be seen. Hamid would have liked him to share this moment but his son had been keeping himself to himself recently, growing more sulky. He had even objected to the move.

'Where will we get the furniture?' said his wife, standing in the middle of the room.

'We'll buy it. Look.' He took out his wallet. It was so fat, it couldn't close.

He found Arif sitting in the car, the radio loud. Hamid turned it down.

'Well, old chap,' he said. 'What do you think?'

'Great,' Arif muttered.

'Earth has not anything to show more fair: . . .'

Hamid stood in the garden. The long, blond grass blew in the wind. It was dusk and he looked up at his home, the fortress where he kept his family safe. A light shone from Arif's attic bedroom – he had insisted on this tiny room, no more than a cupboard up in the roof. Down below were the bedrooms; then, below them, the curtained french windows, glowing bluish from the TV. How solid his house, solid and secure.

Today he wore his tweed suit from Austin Reed. He stood like a squire amidst the swaying weeds.

Summer was ending now, and grass choked the flowerbeds. Neither he nor his wife were proficient in gardening, but that did not stop the pride.

It grew darker. To one side of him rose the block of his house. To the other side, beyond the trees, the sky glowed orange. This side lay London. He thought of his shops casting their own glow over the pavement; he thought of the blood-red neon of THE EMPIRE STORES shining in the night. How ashy those faces seemed, looking up at the window to gaze at the comforts within! Ruined, pasty faces; the losers, the lost, the dispossessed. The walking wounded who once ruled the Empire, pressing their noses against his Empire Stores . . .

He thought of their squalid comforts: those rows of bottles and those magazines showing bald portions of women's bodies. Here at home, on the other hand, he had a mahogany bookcase filled with English classics, all of them bound in leather: Dickens, Shakespeare and the poet he had taken to his own heart: William Wordsworth.

The trees, bulkier now in the night, loomed against the suffused sky. 'Dull would he be of soul who could pass by/A sight so touching in its majesty: . . .'

A chill wind rattled the weeds and blew against his legs. He heard the faint thump of music, if you could call it music, from Arif's window. The long, dry grass blew to and fro in the darkness. He realized that he was shivering.

His wife said she was lonely. She sat in the lounge, its new chairs arranged for conversations, and all day she had the TV on. She talked about Lahore; she said she was homesick. She talked about her sisters, and how they had sat all morning laughing and brushing each other's hair. More and more she talked like this.

'Nobody talks to me here,' she said. 'They get into their cars and drive to their tea parties.'

'You must take driving lessons.'

'The car is so big. It frightens me.'

'Then you must have a tea party here.'

She thought about this for some time. Then she said: 'Who should I invite?'

'The neighbours, of course. And then there are the parents of Arif's schoolfriends.'

'But we don't know the parents of Arif's school-friends.'

'What about that boy, what's his name, Thompson? His father is an executive with Proctor & Gamble.'

'But what shall I cook for them?'

'And that very pleasant couple next door? We've said good morning often enough, and discussed the state of the hedge.'

So it was arranged. A small party for Sunday tea, so that he himself could be present.

For the next week she was restless; she moved about the house, frowning at the furniture and standing back from it, her head on one side. During one evening she moved the settee three times. She took Arif down to Marks & Spencers to buy him a new pair of trousers.

'Christ,' said Arif. 'It's only a bloody tea party.'

'Don't you dare insult your mother!' Hamid's voice was shrill. He, too, moved the settee one more time.

The question of food was vexing. His wife thought sandwiches and cake most suitable. He himself thought she should produce those titbits in which she excelled: pakoras, brinjal fritters and the daintiest of samosas. Nobody cooked samosas like his Sharine.

In the end they compromised. They would have both.

'East meets West,' he joked; his nerves made him high-spirited. He joggled the plaits of Aisha, his youngest daughter; one plait and then the other, and she squealed with pleasure. 'East, West, home's best,' he chanted to her, before she scuttled into the kitchen.

He wanted to tell his family how much he loved

them, and how proud he would be to show them off at the tea party. He wanted to tell them how he had stood in the garden, his heart swelling for them. But his daughters would just giggle; his wife would look flustered . . . And Arif? He no longer knew what Arif would do. He only knew that he himself would feel foolish.

On the Saturday he went into the stock-room of the Empire Stores and fetched some choice items: chocolate fancies, iced Kunzle cakes. There was little demand from his customers for these high-class items. Only the best would do, however, for those who lived in Potters Bar.

It was a cool, blustery evening. There must be a storm blowing up. Kentucky boxes bowled along the pavement. Further up the street a man stood in a doorway, bellowing. It was an eerie sound, scarcely human. Hamid buttoned up his jacket as he left the shop, carrying his parcels. Far down the street he heard the smash of glass: he clutched the parcels to his chest.

Then it happened. He was just getting into the car. As he did so, he chanced to glance back across the street, towards the parade of shops. It was at that moment that the door of the sauna and massage opened and Arif stepped out.

Within him, Hamid's heart shifted like a rock.

He could not move. The face was in shadow; all he could see was the glow of a cigarette. Arif smoking? For some reason this only faintly surprised Hamid.

There the boy stood, a slight figure in that familiar blue and white anorak. He turned to look back at the door; then he turned round and made his way across the road, towards Hamid.

Hamid stood. He opened his mouth to cry out, but nothing happened. Then, as Arif neared him, the street-light fell upon his face.

It was a thinner face; thin, and knowing, and much older than Arif. An unknown, shifty, Englishman's face.

Hamid climbed into his car and fumbled with the key. His hands felt damp and boneless. He told himself to stop being ridiculous; he felt a curious sinking, yet swelling sensation, as if he had aged ten years in the last moments.

Driving home, he tried to shake off his unease. After all, it had been a stranger. Nothing to do with his own cherished son. Why then could he not concentrate on the road ahead? He was a level-headed fellow; he always had been.

Sharine was in a state. 'Where have you been?' she cried.

'It's only ten o'clock,' he said, and asked, alarmed: 'What's happened?'

'What's happened? I've spilt the dahl and dropped the sugar and, oh my nerves.'

She was standing in the kitchen. The air was aromatic with cooking.

'The children have been helping?'

'The girls, yes, until I sent them to bed.'

'Arif?'

She shrugged. 'Him, help me?'

'Where is he?'

'Where he always is.'

Hamid walked up the stairs, up past the first landing, then up the narrow flight of stairs to the attic. For some reason he needed to see his son. He knew he would be there, but he needed to see him.

His heart thumped; it must be those stairs, he was no longer as young as he was. Thud, thud, went Arif's music. Hamid knocked on the door.

'What is it?' Arif's voice was sharp, yet muffled.

'It's your father.'

'Wait.'

A few sounds, then Arif opened the door.

'What do you do in there all evening?' asked Hamid. 'Why don't you help your mother? We have a tea party tomorrow.'

Arif shrugged.

'Why don't you answer my questions?' asked Hamid. 'Why?'

A pause. Arif stood behind the half-open door. Outside, the wind rattled against the slates. Finally he said: 'Why are you so interested?'

Hamid stared. 'And what sort of answer is that?'

'Ask yourself.' Arif slowly scratched the spot on his chin. 'If you have the inclination.'

And he slowly closed the door.

That night there was a storm. The window panes clattered and shook; the very house, his fortress, seemed to shudder. In the morning Hamid found that out in the garden some of the balustrade had fallen down. It was made of the most crumbly concrete.

'Charming,' said Mrs Yates. 'Love the wallpaper, awfully daring. And what sweet little girls.'

Tea cups clinked. Sharine, in her silk sari, moved from one guest to another. Her daughters followed her with plates of cakes. Everything was going like clockwork. Looking at the pleasant faces, Hamid felt a flush of satisfaction. It had all been worth it. The years . . . The work . . .

'And where's the lad?' Mr Thompson asked, jovially.

'He'll be down,' said Hamid, looking at the door and then at his watch. 'Any minute.' Silently, he urged Arif to hurry up.

94

Mr Thompson's wife, whose name Hamid unfortunately had not caught, finished her cup of tea and said: 'Would it be frightfully rude if I asked to see the house?'

Mr Thompson laughed. 'Rosemary, you're incorrigible.'

Other guests stood up, too: Mr and Mrs Yates from next door, old Colonel Tindall from down the road, the teenage girls belonging to the widowed lady opposite.

'A guided tour,' joked Hamid, gathering his scattered wits. 'Tickets please.'

Sharine stood in the middle of the lounge, holding the tea pot. She looked alarmed but he gave her a small, reassuring nod. After all, the house was spick and span.

He led the way. Upstairs he pointed out the view from the master bedroom; the bathroom en suite.

'Carpets everywhere!' said Mrs Yates. 'And what an original colour!'

'Must have cost you,' said Mr Thompson, man to man. Hamid nodded modestly, his face hot with pleasure.

'What's up there?' asked Mrs Yates.

'Just the attic,' said Hamid.

But before he could continue, she had mounted the stairs and Mrs Thompson was following her.

95

'Rosemary!' called Mr Thompson, and turned to Hamid. 'Women!'

Hamid hurried up the stairs. Thud, thud . . . the narrow treads shook, he could hear above him the thump of Arif's music, and then he had arrived at the landing and one of the women was pushing open Arif's door.

'May I?' she turned and asked Hamid.

But by then she had opened the door.

There are some sights that a person never forgets. Sometimes they rise up again in dreams; in his sleep Hamid saw mottled faces, their skin bleeding, pressed up against the glass of his shop. He saw stumps raised, waving in his face, in those long-forgotten alleys in Lahore. All the wreckage of this world, from which he had tried, so very hard, to protect those he loved.

Through his life, which was a long and prosperous one, he never forgot the sight that met his eyes that Sunday afternoon. Arif, sprawled on the bed, his eyes closed. Arif, his own son, snoring as the men snored who lay on the pavements. On the floor lay empty cans of lager and two scattered magazines, their pages open: *Mayfair* and *Penthouse*.

Explosions, riots and wreckage all around the turning world. The small hiss of indrawn breath from the two women who stood beside him.

· *Lost Boys* ·

*M*y husband Ewan once shouted: 'Don't you realize I had a deprived childhood?'

It sounded a wonderful childhood to me, compared to my own upbringing in safe and leafy Kent. His mother was a painter called Lily Frears. You might have heard of her; she was a great success in her day and she was a part of so many lives that she's in the indexes of all those biographies one reads on the train. She'd been a beautiful girl with ruddy skin and bold gypsy eyes. She'd modelled for Augustus John. More than modelled, I suspect. She'd been through two marriages, one to a young sculptor and the other to Ewan's father, a Swiss businessman and patron of the arts. He'd been bemused by her, besotted with her, and had finally died – I said from unrequited love but Ewan says from pancreatitis. Throughout her husbands and lovers she'd kept stubbornly to her original name, her independence, her subtle, dappled paintings and to hand-rolling her own cigarettes from pipe tobacco.

I imagined Ewan, a small boy, perched on the corduroy knees of the eminent painters of the past, most of whom, at some point, had been in love with Lily. In fact I was half in love with her myself. Another thing Ewan once said, only partly joking: 'You married me for my mother.'

'Lots of people loved her.'

He replied: 'The only things she loves are her cats.'

'But you're her son. She must love you.'

'She's vaguely surprised by me now. That she produced this enormous man.' He paused. 'When I was young I just got in the way.'

He said she forgot he was there. Those evenings I imagined – oh how I imagined them, with coarse red wine and passionate beliefs – he remembered just as boring and smoky. He said he'd crawl under the sofa to sleep and the next day he'd miss school. I thought it sounded marvellous. Sometimes she took him to France, or to Tuscany for the summer. Once they lived in a hotel in Cairo for a year; he never knew why.

I called her romantic. He called her untrustworthy. She sent him to boarding school in Sussex. Suddenly she'd turn up during chapel, swathed in a Kashmiri shawl; as he filed out she'd whisk him down to the beach to search for shells. But sometimes on real visiting days he would stand at the gates, all smartened up, and wait, and wait . . . when we were quarrelling he'd tell me this story to make me sorry for him.

She lost him frequently, he said, quoting Oscar Wilde about losing twice seems like carelessness. We live in Hendon (a suburb she always found vaguely comic – she could never remember the number of our house and would send postcards to the wrong address). Above our lounge fire is one of her paintings. I love it. There's drenched green bodies, all naked, sitting under the trees. He remembers when it was painted.

'We'd rented a cottage in the New Forest, and a lot of the grown-ups went swimming, naked, in a river. Afterwards she sat down and painted the others and I wandered off. She forgot me. I was only five. I wandered down the stream and fell in and nearly drowned.' He paused. 'All for that painting. What would you rather, that painting or me?'

'But I've got both.'

He sighed. 'That's just what she would say.'

When I first met Lily she was still lovely – old and bony, but with those large, vague eyes: a face with a Past. Even if she didn't wear her fringed dresses and crimson stockings, people would have gazed with admiration in the street. She lived in a cluttered mansion flat opposite the British Museum and ate in the sandwich bar downstairs. She still taught, part-time, at the Central School of Art, where she had become mythologized in her lifetime, the last of an era. When I was first married I used to visit her and sit for hours, eating salami rolls and listening to her as the day darkened outside and neither of us wanted to break the spell and switch on the lights.

Anyone less like a mother-in-law would be hard to imagine. In fact I felt older than her – the sober, sensible one who voiced objections and wanted her to get the dates right.

Ewan visited her too; not as a treat, however, but as a duty. One day I looked at him: he was thirty and already putting on weight. It was harder nowadays to imagine him as a child.

I said: 'You didn't appreciate her. She's such a free spirit.'

'I didn't want a free spirit,' he said. 'I wanted a mother.'

It all changed, as everything does, when we had children. Alexis arrived, and then Cassandra (the arty names were my choice). I became closed into our house in Hendon and I couldn't get up to

London to see Lily. When I did it was not the same. The children sucked the paintbrushes and tripped over the cat litter trays. Lily bought them charming presents, like a second-hand railway engine, that were far too old for them and had to be put into the cupboard, amidst shrieks, when we got home.

She was always Lily, never Granny. She wouldn't let them call her that because she felt the wings of mortality brushing her face; she said this, touching her rouged cheek.

My own parents' house was, as always, more comfortable and appropriate than Lily's flat. We'd go down for Sunday lunch and the children could toddle across the safe green lawns of my childhood. They loved my mother's fridge, which was always crammed. I thought of Lily's, empty but for a tin of Kit-e-Kat and a half-bottle of gin (I said she was too poor to buy a whole bottle but Ewan said she was too stingy).

At Lily's the only roast beef came in a cellophane roll, but at my parents' there was a proper Sunday lunch with gravy. Ewan always got on well with my parents – better than I do myself – and during the talk about What We're Doing to the House (a perennial topic) I found myself disloyally yearning for Lily, who'd never owned anything in her life.

When Alex was three he tried to sip the sherry, and when reprimanded he said: 'Lily lets me.'

My mother looked at him. 'Well, Granny doesn't.'

By the time Alex was four, a small, grave boy and the image of his father, and Cassie was eighteen months, Lily had become distanced into a golden ideal of freedom. It seemed as hard to reach that as to walk into her green, forest painting above our mantelpiece. Ewan thought I was a wonderful mother but then he didn't know what domesticity was like, he only came home to it. Arms full of damp Babygros, sometimes I felt like screaming.

What was I like; where had I gone? I felt emptied, an empty vessel, drained by others' needs. I wanted to be myself, like Lily.

Ewan said: 'She should never have had me. She wasn't a natural mother. You are.'

I said sharply: 'How do you know?'

Mentally I added up the weeks – yes, weeks – since we had made love. And then how had it been? Functional, courteous.

Dull.

I thought: life's passing me by. It never passed Lily by. She *lived*.

One hot June day, on impulse, I took the children up to London and rang Lily's bell. Kissing her papery cheek, I realized how strongly I'd been missing her.

'You say you like surprises.'

'My dear girl,' she said. 'We shall go swimming.'

We took a taxi up to Hampstead Heath and walked along a grassy path, through a meadow. The grass and cow parsley were taller than Alex. Bees murmured, or was it the drone of cars? The city seemed far away as we walked along our enchanted path. Hendon dwindled. I hadn't been to the Heath for years; I didn't realize it was so wild. I felt drunk with the scent of flowers.

Finally we arrived at a hedge, fenced with railings. In front of us was an open gate.

'I've been coming here for ever,' said Lily. 'First I'd swim, then I'd draw the bathers. It's ladies only – the Ladies' Lake.'

The Ladies' Lake . . . even the name sounded mysterious. Behind the hedge I could hear faint laughter: I could see a glint of water. I never knew such a pond existed; the splashings through the hedge had the charmed inevitability of a dream.

We only had Lily's costume – an odd, shiny, red garment – and besides, children weren't allowed, so one of us had to wait in the meadow with them. Lily picked two grass-heads and I drew out the short one, so she disappeared first through the gate – a tall, striding figure, despite her age. She wore a straw hat and a faded orange dress. She looked so young from the back that it was a shock when she turned to wave.

She seemed to be gone for hours, but that afternoon time had no importance. Cassie had fallen asleep in the push-chair. I sat with Alex amongst the tall grasses, nibbling sorrel leaves and trying to persuade him to take off his T-shirt. Like his Dad, he preferred to be fully dressed.

'We used to bathe naked,' said Lily, sitting down beside me and passing me the swimming costume. 'Or did I just imagine it?' Her face looked damp and bare and old with the make-up washed off.

'Will you be all right?' I asked, looking at them as I left. 'Try to take Alex's clothes off.'

What followed was the most beautiful half-hour I think I've ever spent. Slipping into the water, warm and murky as soup, was like slipping into one of Lily's paintings. The heavy horse-chestnuts cast a dappled shade, and on the banks lay sunbathing women, some bare-breasted. No cocksure, competitive men, no loud boys showing off, no children with their whines and needs . . . Just silence as women swam lazily to and fro, each alone, each free. It was hard to believe we were just a few miles from Leicester Square; it could have been the New Forest. I could be Lily, swimming twenty years before . . .

I swam slowly, gazing at my bare arms, blurred and yellowed in the water . . . The water weeds brushed my legs, like drowned women. Far above, a plane passed. It made no noise, it was irrelevant. I imagined it packed with businessmen. Ewan was taking the Glasgow shuttle that day – like his mother, Ewan is in paint; in his case, however, it's the Marketing Division of ICI. I thought that of all the people I knew, only Lily would have brought me here.

I dried myself luxuriously, taking my time. Then I got dressed and walked barefoot down the cinder path towards the gate. I remember my exact sensations during that walk. My damp hair tickled my shoulders; my limbs felt refreshed and elastic, my body felt alive for the first time . . . oh, for years. I wondered how I'd feel if I had a lover whom I could tell these things, and who wouldn't think I was being self-indulgent. No – who wouldn't need telling – who would know.

Through the hedge I could see the orange blur of Lily's dress. The last thing I remember thinking was: the children are quiet.

Lily was sitting still. It took me a moment to realize she had an open pad and she was drawing Cassie.

I walked nearer and looked down, over the henna'd streaks of Lily's drying hair, at the delicate lines of my child's face on the paper.

'Can't get that waxiness,' murmured Lily. 'Not

with a pencil.' She paused. 'Such exquisite little objects ... I've always preferred them asleep, don't you?'

I smiled, then I looked around. 'Where's Alex?'

Silence. Lily was just shading in the mouth.

'Hmm?' she said. 'He was here a minute ago.'

'Where is he?' The sharp note in my voice frightened me.

'Oh, I know. He said he was looking for bottle tops.'

'Was it just a minute?'

I straightened up and looked around. To one side was the hedge. On all the other sides stretched the meadow, full of tall grass. Far away stood some trees, with people walking and picnicking.

'Alex?' I called.

I waited. Silence, except for a splash in the lake.

'Alex!'

Nothing moved except the breeze, which blew gently over the meadow, silvering the grasses. Swathes of them rippled, and then were still. I waited. The breeze blew again, chilling me. The grass moved, the cow parsley swayed, its white heads bobbing and bouncing, and then was still.

'Alex!'

I swung round. 'Lily, you go that way.' I pointed in one direction, then I tried to unbuckle Cassie. She woke with a yell. My hands wouldn't work;

I fumbled with the push-chair buckle. Finally I wrenched it open and grabbed her. I bundled her under one arm and plunged into the grass, in the opposite direction to Lily.

The meadow was so huge; I'd never realized Hampstead Heath was this size. It was bumpy, too; it was difficult to run, stumbling over the hidden potholes with Cassie bouncing and shrieking.

'*Alex!*'

The sun had slid behind a cloud and the Heath looked sinister. How could I have believed in the happy freedom of my swim? How could I have been so foolish? Why had I left an old, vague, self-absorbed lady in charge of my most precious possessions? How could I?

Tears blurred my eyes as I struggled through the weeds – they were weeds, wicked weeds, trying to trip me up. As I neared them, the trees looked loomingly black and heavy.

People stopped to stare. 'Have you seen a little boy?' I screeched. They shook their heads and I hated them for being in the wrong place; but I hated myself more.

Far away I could see the orange blur of Lily. I thought: you stupid old woman.

If this has ever happened to you, then you know those pictures that crowd your head and that you'd never allowed yourself to see. You'll know how time literally ceases.

How long it took I'll never remember. But when I saw that small, blue and white figure, he was standing beside the gate, right back at the place we'd left. He was standing waiting for us, my lost boy, and his face was red.

Lost boys. I pictured Ewan, a little boy in his school blazer, waiting at the school gates for a mother who never arrived.

Ewan once said: 'I never had a childhood. Know why? Because *she* was the child.'

I never told Ewan what had happened, though Alex in his usual matter-of-fact way said that he'd only found two bottle tops. But after that, for the first time in his life, he slept for fourteen hours solid.

Eight years have passed since that day. Lily's dead now. But I remember it because this morning Alex, now twelve years old, asked me about the drawing of Cassie we have in the lounge, above my desk. (I run my own small business now, oh yes I've done something.) It's a beautiful drawing and I like looking at it when I'm working out my VAT . . . That sleeping, waxen face from a past era, years that were suffocating, and often painful, but which I'll never forget.

Alex asked me, and I told him about that day and what happened. He couldn't remember anything about it. And for the first time I tried to tell him exactly what Lily was like. I said that in fact she was not such a famous painter, just an artistic woman who had some doting patrons. That she wasn't a living legend at the art school, but that they'd kept her on out of kindness. That when I first met her I resented my parents and compared them to her in a way that did justice to neither. That idolizing her hurt my husband, because he knew the truth. (I doubt if Alex took this in, but I went on in a rush.) That people sometimes giggled at her in the street, but that I was sure others saw the ruined, striking beauty of her face.

That she was utterly herself, a true original; that she had time for me when nobody else noticed I needed it. And that there was nobody I would rather see walking through the door at this moment.

I said all this, and more, because I wanted him to know her. To idolize anyone is the worst thing one can do, because then they are lost to us.

Then I said that for the price of that drawing of Cassie I might have lost him. But he pushed me away. He's like his father; he hates soppy stuff.

· *Stiff Competition* ·

I knew I shouldn't have gone to the Fathers' Class. Well, would you? Perhaps you're the pseudy participating type. Perhaps you're one of those gonad-less *Guardian* readers who talks about growing with your wife. There's plenty moved in round our way; they never close their blinds so you can see what sharing lives they're leading, him at the sink, her working on her gender grievances. There's always those corduroy sag-bags on the floor, where they talk things through.

I don't. When they're exposed to the frank air, all those little mysteries wither away, don't they? Well, in this class we'd learn how to breathe them through. Breathe her, the wife, through childbirth, that is. Angie said it was all about facing one's emotions. I'd faced mine; they told me I didn't want to go. But I wasn't allowed to face that particular one. Illogical eh?

We'd all have to lie down on cushions; that's what she said. I'd feel a right berk.

But I had to go. She didn't tell me to, of course. She just exerted that familiar old pressure, like a thin iron band slowly tightening round my skull. We've had it about my smoking and the way it's always her who phones her parents (well they're her parents aren't they?), and the way she always has to phone mine (well?). And how I hadn't opened the Mothercare catalogue she'd left on my desk. It's got worse since she's been expecting.

So we went. We were going to go up in the lift but it said MAXIMUM 8 PERSONS and there were already eight women in it, all massively pregnant.

'Tut tut,' I told them, pointing to the sign. 'Tut tut, ladies.'

Their heads turned slowly, like a herd of cows. They didn't get it.

As we climbed the stairs Angie sighed. 'I wish you wouldn't get facetious,' she said. 'Just because you're nervous.'

'I wasn't facetious. Just accurate.'

She was starting to pant. 'You find it a threat, don't you,' she puffed. 'This sort of thing.'

I didn't answer because by now I was puffed too. Must be all those fags.

Upstairs Angie disappeared on her hundredth daily visit to the loo. I went into the room.

116

There were rows of chairs facing a screen, and a giant, unpleasant-looking plastic object on a plinth. Amongst the vast women sat their small men; they wore that smug look people have when doing their duty, you see it on drivers when they pull in to let a fire-engine pass, or voters emerging from a polling-booth. What a load of wets. I'd seen a promising-looking pub opposite the hospital. I wondered how many of these blokes wished they were sitting there with a pint of Fullers in front of them. I wondered how many of them admitted it.

I sat down next to an inoffensive, bespectacled chap.

'Sorry,' he said. 'This seat's taken.'

I sat one seat further away. There was something familiar about that voice. I looked at him again.

'Bugger me,' I said. 'It's Condom.'

He stared at me. Then he said: 'Nobody's called me that for fifteen years.'

'Who'm I then?'

His eyes narrowed. 'You look awfully familiar . . .'

'Go on. Guess.'

It took him ages. Finally he said slowly: 'It's not . . . Slatterly?'

I nodded.

'Sorry,' he said. 'I didn't recognize you.'

'You're looking at my gut? Married, aren't I? That's a Married gut.'

There was one of those pauses. What the hell could we say?

So I volunteered. 'Here we are then, back in school.'

He paused, and his Adam's apple moved up and down: 'Older, wiser, but still with a lot to learn.'

What a prig! He'd always been one, of course. Edward Codron . . . Condom. His nickname had been laughably unsuitable. Once we'd been in the cloakroom, four of us, engaged in what we called Stiff Competition. I won't go into details but the general gist was that first one to fill a matchbox won. Anyway, creepy Condom came in and would you believe he reported us to the Head? You didn't do that sort of thing.

Still, he and I had been kind of friends – not mates, friends – because we lived in the same street. Anglepoise Mansions, I called his house, both his parents being professors.

'Lots to catch up on,' I said. 'Bet you went to university.'

He nodded. 'Jesus.'

'Pardon?'

'Jesus, Cambridge. And you?'

I shook my head. 'Insurance.'

He wore a cord jacket, Hush Puppies and a badge saying PROTEST AND SURVIVE.

I said: 'Bet you teach in a poly.'

'How did you guess?'

'I can tell.' Another pause. Then I said: 'One thing I needn't ask you . . .' I gestured at the other couples. 'If you got married.'

He coughed. I remembered his little cough. 'Actually we're not. We're living together.'

Now what the hell can you reply to that? I glared at him. Weedy old Condom, eh? By A-levels he was the only one in the history group who hadn't got his leg over. Well, who'd admitted it. After all, Bayliss used to frequently show us a different pack-of-threes, but I'd always suspected he'd just rotated them. Devious bastard. He ended up a barrister.

The hall was filling. I gazed furtively at Condom. He'd not only impregnated, but illegally. There's something irritatingly highly sexed, isn't there, about unmarried couples. Compared to married ones.

As if on cue, Angie came in. She sat down, lowering her weight with a sigh.

'Meet the wife,' I said.

'I have a name.'

'This is Angie,' I said. 'And this is Condom.'

'Edward Codron.' He leaned over to shake her hand.

They had one of those conversations about where are you living now? Condom, thank God, lived miles

from us. How was he going to introduce his what's-
her-name, when she arrived? If he didn't, how would
I? Lover? Partner? Life-Comrade? I resented him
having to make me decide, just because he wanted
to make some social bloody statement.

Come to think of it, he'd always done things thor-
oughly; doggedly carrying them through. He'd been
a terrible swot. Nobody admitted they crammed for
exams, except him. He didn't even drink. And there
was I, numbed with hangover in assembly, 'Oh
Come, Emmanuel' hitting my head like a gong.
The wickedest thing he played was chess. I thought:
bet he drives one of those neutered little Citroëns,
putter-putter, that I'm always getting stuck behind.

'What was he like at school?' asked Angie, indicating me.

'Terry? He wore winklepickers. He was a real
tearaway.'

'No!' Angie gazed at me.

'Don't look so surprised,' I said.

'He smoked Players Untipped,' said Condom.
'Quite a Jack the Lad.'

'Really?'

Her look annoyed me. I said: 'I went out with
the birds from the art school. Twiggy eyelashes . . .
thick white lipstick . . . long thighs . . .'

'I painted on my lashes with charcoal,' said Angie.
'I remember now.'

'You didn't.'

'You didn't know me then,' she said. 'You don't know what I was like. You've never asked.'

'Course I have.'

'You haven't.' She paused, then smiled. 'And just look at us now.'

'This is what you did it for,' I said.

'What?' asked Condom.

'This,' I said, gesturing round. 'Reproduction.'

Then a woman came into the room. She was a gigantic creature in one of those Indian tents that liberated, fat women wear. She started to chat to us, and introduced the plastic thing which she called, with a simper, Pauline the Pelvis. Everyone sat in solemn silence. I remembered our Biology classes, fifteen years before . . . The raucous giggles, our teacher stuttering. But we were older now; we'd put our matchboxes behind us. Today nobody laughed.

In fact Angie was holding my hand – there, in front of everybody. She had called this an important moment for us both. I watched Pauline the Pelvis being tilted back and forward and thought of all the pelvises, or pelvi, I must have known, unbeknownst to me.

By now the tent was burbling on about relationships, and how the birth process was about bonding, and opening up to each other. I thought:

they've opened. I pictured, with longing, a pint. A bag of dry-roasted peanuts. Nobody talks about relationships in pubs.

'Your hand's clammy,' Angie whispered.

'S'not mine, it's yours.'

'Terry, don't be tense.'

It was then that they opened the cupboards and started taking out the cushions.

'They're not for us as well?' I hissed. 'The blokes?'

'Of course. That's the point.'

'Can't we just watch?'

It was at that moment, when my mouth had opened for the next sentence, that the door opened and Sue walked in.

I froze; it was her. It was Sue. Her blonde hair was curly now; her smock billowed in the breeze from the fan and she was walking straight towards me.

'Ouch!' whispered Angie. 'You're hurting.'

I let go her hand. Sue came nearer.

'Darling,' she whispered to Condom, 'have I missed a lot?'

Her face looked scrubbed; her skin bleached and freckly. Those light-blue eyes . . . She looked cleaner, and older, and even more beautiful.

She sat down beside me, hip to hip. You know the saying: his bowels turned to water? Mine felt like that. At any moment she would recognize me. She mustn't.

Sue, of all girls. *Sue.* I kept my face turned away.

I was gazing straight into Angie's eyes. 'What's the matter?' she whispered.

'Nothing.'

'We'll all be doing it together. You needn't be worried.'

'Me, worried?'

Chairs scraped as everybody stood up. I tried to escape but Condom tapped my shoulder. 'This is Susan,' he said.

She said 'Hello' before she met my eye. Then she said: 'Good grief.'

Condom said: 'You knew each other?'

She paused. 'Briefly. Slightly.'

'Terry was just talking about girls from the art school.' He turned to her. 'But you've never mentioned him.'

She smiled. 'We hardly knew each other.'

My shirt was sticking to my armpits. Now we were all walking over to the cushions. I tried to nudge Angie towards the far corner but Sue and Condom were behind us, and when we were told to lie down we all lay down together. Angie on one side of me; Sue the other.

The Indian tent picked its way amongst us, smiling down. 'First we have to relax. I know this may seem strange to some of you . . . We'll be doing First-Stage breathing . . . Deep breaths, one, two, three . . .'

In the corner of my eye I could see the dome of Sue's belly. Stretched out beside me, she was breathing heavily, in and out, as instructed. I could smell her perfume.

Sue and me, lying beside the gas fire. I'd got the living, breathing Sue in my arms. Her suede mini-skirt up around her waist . . . her leg wrapped around me . . . and my hand sliding down through the elastic waistband of her tights . . . we were rolling over, bumping against the fender . . .

'OK? Relaxed? She's fully dilated by now, and moving into the Second Stage of labour . . . Time for the shallow pants.'

Sue, panting in my ear . . . the rasp of her tights as she rearranged her limbs . . . she'd done this before. After all, she was an art-school girl . . .

'Can I?' *My voice was husky; I had to clear my throat.* 'Can I?'

I squeezed my eyes tight shut. Around me, rising and falling, they were panting *en masse*.

'Can I?'

'Yes.'

But could I?

'The contractions are coming on stronger now, keep panting, with each wave . . . Each wave growing more and more powerful . . .'

Crouched over myself, I was lumbering to my feet to switch off the light . . . behind me she lay waiting, glowing in the firelight . . . I was fumbling for my wallet.

A whisper. 'Can I help?'

'Help by rubbing,' said the voice. 'Rubbing her back, Dads. Help by breathing with her, breathing her through . . . Now she needs your support . . .'

Crouched there, my trousers round my ankles. I kept my back to her. Silence. I could hear her breathing behind me, waiting.

Stealthy, crackling sounds. My hands big and useless as sausages. And there it lay, dwindled . . .

I sat, hunched like a miser over my humiliating little offering.

'She's needing reassurance now, Dads. The contractions are much, much stronger . . .'

'You all right?' she asked.

Untruthfully, I nodded.

She put her arms around me. 'You've done this before?'

A pause. Then, untruthfully, I nodded again.

She set to work, tender and deft. Tenderly she tried, with her warm hands.

No bloody good.

All those matchboxes . . . all those sessions in our Arctic toilet . . . and in my creaking bed, through the wall the answering scrape-scrape of my sister's hamster going round its wheel. And when it came to it . . .

'Terry.'

A hand touched my arm. I jerked upright. Angie was sitting up, so were the others. I heard grunts as the women got to their feet.

Angie dusted down my suit, and smiled. 'You did it marvellously. Sounded as if *you* were having the baby, not me.' She paused. 'Wasn't so bad, was it?'

Behind my head I heard Sue murmuring to Condom. Was she telling him about it now? Or would she save it till later, for the togetherness time on their corduroy sag-bags? Some things are best left unsaid . . . But you can bet they'd talk *this* through.

Laugh it through, more like.

'It's the film now,' Angie said. '*Tamsin is Born.*' She paused: 'Where are you going?'

'I'll wait in the pub.'

She pulled me back. 'Terry, don't feel threatened. I've seen it before, it's terrifically moving.'

'Well, I'm moving terrifically fast.'

'Darling – look, it's no reflection on your masculinity or anything if you find it a bit overwhelming. Nobody will mind.'

'I'll faint,' I said. 'I'm off.'

But just then the lights were extinguished and it was too late. Grey numbers wobbled on the screen and I was trapped. The film began, in startling technicolor.

And when tiny, red Tamsin was born, shall I tell you what happened?

Condom passed out. He did, no kidding. There was this scrape, as his chair tipped over.

Later, in the pub, I said: 'Fancy old Condom fainting.'

Angie gazed at me over her orange juice. 'You're smiling.'

'I'm not.'

'Why? Why this macho power-game, this stupid competitiveness? What are you afraid of?'

I shrugged genially. I was well into my second pint, Jesus, it tasted good. I lit my third fag. I felt better. She couldn't get at me now.

Then she spoilt it. She sighed and said: 'Your nice friend, what's-his-name?'

'Condom.'

'Edward. He doesn't behave like that.' She gazed at me. Around my skull the band tightened.

'Behave like what?'

'Behave as if he's frightened of failing.' She paused, then she said: 'Real men don't.'

· Horse Sense ·

*W*hen I first moved to the estate my only companions were Terry Wogan and a horse. Terry was just on the radio, but the horse was real enough. It was a big brown thing that lived in a field at the end of my garden. I'm not used to horses but soon it was hanging its heavy head over my fence and I was feeding it chapatis. At first it alarmed me, baring its slimy yellow teeth, stained like a smoker's.

I come from London. So does my husband. But we moved to this place near Swindon because it's Silicon Valley and he was making his way in the world. I was proud of him then.

The estate was full of children. They passed fast on their skate-boards; their laughter made my chest hurt. Sometimes, waiting for the bus, there would be a little girl standing in front of me and I felt weak, from wanting to touch her hair.

The neighbours weren't really unfriendly. We just

didn't have that much in common, me having no kids. I don't think it was to do with prejudice – after all, I didn't go around in a sari or anything. I was born and bred in England, the same as them. We didn't perform weird rites. The only thing Ranjit worshipped was the silicon chip.

I talked to the horse when I was hanging out my washing. It might have looked funny otherwise. I had these one-way conversations behind the flapping sheets. I told it what I was cooking for dinner, and what was going on in *EastEnders*. One day I said to it, quite distinctly: 'I think I'm going mad.'

That was the day I had been to the shoe shop in Swindon and made such a fool of myself. The horse went on eating, of course, and flicked away a fly.

I should have told my husband but he didn't like disturbance. He's older than me – he had been a bachelor for years and his family had started to despair. The grey flecks in his hair gave him a weighty look, as if he had deeper thoughts than me. So I cooked and cleaned the house – when he saw a smeary surface he cleared his throat – and, before the panics got too bad, I took the bus into Swindon and went to Marks & Spencers. I had been married two years.

I'm probably making him sound unattractive. I knew I would. But he was kind. He was always buying me gadgets for the kitchen. Have you tried a microwave? I only used it once, and after that I pretended. He would spear a baked potato and pronounce: 'Ten minutes. A miracle.' I would lower my eyes; in marriage you learn to be silent.

He liked things with digital numbers; our house bleeped like a space-ship. He fiddled with the video recorder and indexed all our tapes. From the back I could see the small boy he once was. I wanted to touch him then, but he only handled me in the dark. And then, according to the statistics in my *Woman's Own* survey, not often.

But I didn't mention that, even to myself. I told myself I was lucky. He didn't drink like other men, coming home to a burnt dinner and an irked wife. He kept himself in trim. He never lost his temper. He gave me generous amounts of housekeeping each week. I tell myself these things, and I tell them to you. I don't like to talk of them.

I'll tell you about the horse. It meant a lot to me. Silly, wasn't it? But I stroked its neck and it blew into my hair. We were two lonely creatures together. My husband worked late; he was one of the marketing managers of a computer firm. Under my hand, the horse breathed.

I'll tell you what happened in Lilley & Skinners. I went into Swindon to buy a pair of shoes. A woman was there, with her child. He was a small boy, aged about six, and he wanted blue trainers. But she wanted him to have the red ones, and then he started crying and she slapped him. That was all. And I burst into tears.

I felt such a fool. I had to leave the shop. It was such a small thing, wasn't it? I felt a fool.

Soon after that, it was a cold day in spring; the field was empty. The horse was gone. For a silly moment I thought I had told it too many secrets. The field was bare, with just the dents where its hooves had stood; pitted mud around my back fence. And a week later the bulldozers arrived and they ploughed up the field and started building a service station.

So there was only Terry Wogan left but he was on the telly now; he had his own chat show and instead of talking to me there he was, making film stars simper. It wasn't the same.

I should have got out more. With the warm weather starting, other women went off to garden centres and MFI. People talked about a local beauty spot – a hill with the shape of a white horse cut out in it. Standing there, they said, you could see three counties. But now, just thinking about the bus made my heart thump. I was getting worse.

I had these panics when I got to Swindon. It happened in supermarkets; in Sainsbury's I'd break out in sweat. I couldn't think what to choose. Little tins suddenly made me sad. I'd fumble in my bag for my wallet – it wasn't there, I'd forgotten it, I'd forgotten my keys. What could I possibly choose to buy? How could I want all that stuff? And why? Wasn't everybody looking at me?

I kept glancing at my watch and worrying I'd miss the bus. I'd hurry to the bus station; there were so many buses, so many numbers. Sometimes they would roll the numbers around on the departure boards, losing me. It was the central depot, and though I knew my queue I pictured the wrong bus being there, or my own bus just leaving. However early I turned up, my stomach churned.

I didn't tell Ranjit. He always seemed to be doing something else. Besides, I didn't want to worry him when he was working so hard. They were about to launch a new product, he said, and he was often away overnight – he had to give pep talks, he said, to his countrywide network of sales executives. He spent more and more time, too, working late.

It was best not to speak. If I spoke I would alarm myself; once I made it real, into words, I would start panicking, in earnest.

Then one day I lost my nerve and missed the bus altogether. For a week I had been putting off going into Swindon; just outside the estate, next to the newly-built filling station, there was a parade of shops and I'd been going there. I could do that quite easily – no timetables, no countdowns: just a short walk, whenever I felt like it, quite calmly. No problem with that.

But I needed some upholstery fabric. Days went by and I made excuses to myself, delaying things until the last bus had gone and it was too late. Finally, on the Friday, I did make it to the bus stop. But when the bus arrived, I flunked it and went back home.

The next Monday I did something that was out of character. We all do that on occasion, don't we? That morning I picked up the phone book, found a number and ordered myself a mini-cab.

And look where it led me. My advice: don't do anything that surprises yourself. There's a good reason why you've never done it before.

Eric was the name of the driver and we got to know each other well. He was more responsive than either the horse or Terry. I could talk to the back of his neck, which was red.

The first journey he talked all the way about his late wife. I think he was lonely.

'There was fields here then,' he said, nodding at the passing discount centres. 'She grew up on a farm; all the fields they were yellow with cowslips.' A lorry, hooting, passed us. 'It's an ancient bit of country, this. Those chalk hills, see, far over there? The oldest bit of land for miles.'

I agreed politely, though I couldn't see how one bit of country could be older than another. I was wondering if I dared tell Ranjit about the mini-cab. He would think me so odd. I would take the money out of the housekeeping and he might never notice.

'Money, money,' Eric went on. 'Nobody doesn't have any respect for the land. Plough it up, concrete it over, bung all those little boxes on it. There was a song once: "Little boxes and they all look just the same".'

'They're not,' I said. 'Ours has a through-lounge – some of them have a separate dining-room.' I liked my house.

'One huge suburb,' he went on, 'full of foreigners.' He looked in the driving mirror. 'Begging your pardon.'

'I know,' I said. 'Most of us come from London.'

He must have been about sixty. He talked about the days when he was courting as if it was yesterday. He said it felt like that. He said there was a big harvest supper and his wife-to-be was there, and how they had horses then to pull the carts. Being a town boy, he said, he was alarmed by their huge feet.

While he talked, I thought how in a mini-cab

I didn't feel so panic-stricken, though I still felt twinges: should I tip him? Would he pick me up outside Marks & Spencers at the right time? He did.

The weeks went by and I realized I was looking forward to our trips. His neck got browner in the sun. He said he subscribed to *Psychic News* and that he still talked to his wife. She wasn't really gone. To him, she wasn't. He said his house was on a steep hillside and in the evening, when the place was in shadow and he came through the front door, he heard her voice. She always seemed to be in the next room, but when he got there, the house was silent.

'Do you have any children?' I asked him.

He shook his head.

Outside the window the suburbs of Swindon passed. As I looked out at the industrial warehouses I thought of Ranjit, pyjama'd in the dark. Did he dream?

I said to Eric: 'Last night I dreamed I was in a plane but it wouldn't take off. It just bumped through the streets, faster and faster. Its wings battered at the houses; it made such a mess. I was scared to death. I was sitting inside it; all the passengers were rolling about but it wouldn't go up in the air. There was somebody next to me and he was telling me to open a parcel. The plane

was lurching around; he forced me to open it. I
didn't want to. Inside the parcel – it was made
of old newspapers – inside it there was something
moving.'

I didn't tell him there was a baby inside. To tell
the honest truth, I don't think he was listening.

I do blush, though, when I think of the things I told
Eric. The stuffy car made me careless and I just
spoke to the back of his neck. I told him about my
funny turns, and how I would speak to the furniture.
It didn't seem so odd when there he was conversing
with his dead wife. At least the washing machine
was solid. 'Can you cope with all these sheets?' I
would ask it. 'I've never fancied this pink shirt of
Ranny's. It makes him look like a disc jockey.' At
first it surprised me, hearing, in my empty home,
my own high voice. But once you've been doing it
for a while it seems quite normal. And at least I
wasn't speaking into thin air.

I told him how I'd stand in the middle of a shop
and suddenly feel so empty – a sort of scraped-out,
hurting hollow – and I'd go up the escalators and
buy three belts. I knew I would never wear them,
they didn't go with any of my clothes. But I would
bundle them into the back of my cupboard and keep
them safe.

Ranjit wouldn't have minded the expense – I

told you he was generous – but he would have been worried. Eric was restful because nothing surprised him.

I said: 'Yesterday I burst into tears, thinking of all the chickens that must have died to make me live.'

Eric just replied: 'Once chickens tasted like chickens. Now they're pumped full of hormones.' No wonder I could talk.

It was the hottest summer for years. At night I slept badly, dreaming of horses and slippery slopes. I was helpless; often the plane or carriage in which I was travelling was out of control. I heard trees creak as we knocked against them; banging along the streets, I heard the breaking masonry. Sometimes Ranjit appeared – an altered, panting Ranjit. His hands were rude, and he pulled my skirt up over my head and did such things to me, front and rear, that at breakfast I couldn't meet his eye.

Inside, the house was stifling. The garden was both too stuffy and too exposed – have you ever felt that? While Ranjit slept I stood on the lawn listening to the hum of the motorway. The filling station blared at me, close; its Texaco sign hurt my eyes – it reminded me of my childhood when I had dared myself to look at the sun. I hid behind the shed, where none of the houses could see me, and I gazed at the orange sky above Swindon. I pictured cows and wives buried under concrete and wondered if I would ever have a child. I thought suddenly: am I having a nervous breakdown? Is this the beginning of it? Perhaps I'm one of those housewives I read about in the newspaper. Inside, beside the bed, emerald numbers flipped on our digital clock, telling me that at least something was in order.

The weather grew stifling, as if somebody had closed the doors on England. Towns, cities, old and new hills – they were all one room. I found it more and more difficult to sleep. At first I thought it was the thunder; each evening it rumbled, way beyond the hills I had never visited. But then I realized why I felt uneasy. Ranjit was looking at me.

I would see him out of the corner of my eye; I would catch sight of him reflected in the glass-fronted cabinet. His eyes were on me. I behaved as normal but I started to sweat. I thought: he knows something's wrong.

The next Thursday Eric took me to Sainsbury's. The sky was grey, and weighed down on the car. I felt so faint I nearly asked him to stop, but that would have alarmed me so I just leaned near the open window and tried to concentrate on the

passing buildings . . . Everest Double Glazing . . .
Little Chef . . . Elite Used Cars. When we arrived
at Sainsbury's it was busy and I felt the familiar
fluttering. So I sat still for a moment and held the
door handle.

Then I spoke. I said: 'Does it frighten you?'
'Pardon?'
I didn't reply. I meant: does it frighten you, that
it seems normal to talk to your wife? But then I
realized, as he settled himself in the driver's seat
and lit his pipe, that he considered himself the sane
one in a world that was mad.

Later, when I unpacked my shopping, I found
all sorts of packets that were new to me – frozen
scampi, assorted Elastoplast. I couldn't remember
buying them. My face heated up and my mouth
went dry. I thought: yes, I am mad. I'm mad and
I'll have to tell Ranjit. What will he do with me?

And then, as I lifted out a jar of pickled onions, I
realized I had simply got someone else's shopping
by mistake. Someone, somewhere, was looking at
alien chicken quarters and feeling just the same
way as me.

For a moment I didn't feel lonely. Standing there
beside the fridge I laughed out loud, until the noise
I made frightened me.

Some nights later I was lying on my side looking at

the street light glowing through the curtains. Beside me Ranjit slept. It was four o'clock; I felt damp and restless. My dreams had been disturbing and I was trying to calm myself by measuring the distance between the tulips on the curtains. Far away, a dog barked. I could hear my own heart thumping; these stupid panics were worse at night.

Then I turned my head and froze. Ranjit was lying there with his eyes open.

I don't know why it gave me such a shock. Straight away he closed his eyes; this made it worse. After a moment I touched his shoulder, but he started breathing deeply, as if he were asleep. He couldn't be – he knew that; I knew that.

Suddenly I felt cold. I turned away and pretended to sleep. That dog went on barking; it sounded like somebody sawing through bones, on and on. I thought, for the first time: perhaps it's not just me who's mad.

A place gets to you. Even in our ultra-modern estate it got to me. I had never really listened to Eric and he'd never listened to me, but what he said seeped through, or maybe it was that unsettling midsummer air. All those digital bleeps couldn't reason away the uneasiness I felt in this foreign countryside. Because it was a strange place. Despite its motorways and its Happy Eaters it was pulling at me. Or perhaps the pulling came from inside.

Whatever the reason, the next time I had to take a trip into Swindon – I was going to change my library books, though I hadn't read them all – the next time I said to Eric, as we drove away past Elite Used Cars: 'It's too hot. Let's go somewhere else.'

To tell the truth I didn't mind where we went. My hands stuck to the carrier-bag of books; my torpor made me bold. I just wanted some air. I remember exactly what I was wearing – my yellow C & A dress – and I remember Eric, who was never surprised, taking a right turn at the roundabout, with a car hooting behind him, and saying that if I'd never gone there before I ought to see the famous beauty spot. He started going on about local superstitions, and how ancient it all was and how you could see three counties from up there. But my eyes were closed and my mouth tasted last night's dreams – they caught me off my guard each day; they rose in my throat.

The drive took ages. I started to worry about the money and then I must have dozed off. Blurred, my horse was leaning over my garden fence and talking to me, its jaw working like a horse in a pantomime. It was blurred because I was jolting in the car, just like my dreams when I was jolted along in planes, and I started to feel queasy. And then I opened

my eyes and we were driving up a narrow, bumpy
lane and above me there was a hill, bleached in
the sunlight. The sky was a block of blue above it.
Somebody was talking but it was Eric, and he was
asking me if I could see the horse carved out of the
chalk but we were close up now, and all I could see,
between the bushes, was a large dingy-white gap in
the grass, too wide to recognize. He was saying they
had once worshipped that horse, in pagan times. I
felt sick; I wanted to go home. I didn't know how
long I had slept or whether it should strike me
as odd to take a mini-cab on a joy-ride, except it
didn't feel joyful. I was too far from home; I would
never find my way back. I wanted my kitchen, and
my front door closed behind me. I wanted to be
busy unpacking carrier-bags. My heart fluttered. I
wanted it to be a safe weekday, or as safe as I could
make it.

I don't know if I thought all this then, but I do
know that I was already feeling tight and headachy,
the panic swelling, long before I saw the glint of
Ranjit's car.

In front of me was a chalky car park, with litter
bins. I remember it exactly – that swift moment
when I glanced around – even though all this
happened a year ago. A few empty cars were parked
there; not many, it was a Wednesday lunchtime. But
there was another car parked in the far corner, apart

145

from them, and for a moment I thought idly: a white Escort, just like his.

Eric was asking me something but I didn't hear. We bumped across the car park, closer now. I told myself it was only one head in there, not two. The sunlight flashed against the rear window; I told myself I must be mistaken. I wanted to go home.

But Eric was driving nearer, and now I was telling myself: they're just looking at the view. That's why their heads are so close together. And then we were close up and I saw what they were doing. And then my head was down between my knees and I was saying to Eric *take me home*.

The sunlight blinded me. As we bumped down the track I squeezed my eyes shut. Eric never knew anything was wrong.

I might have understood, if it was a woman. In fact, in some way deep down I had expected it. But not a man. I hadn't expected a man.

When we got home I told Eric to wait outside. I hurried in.

It's surprising, once you look around a place for the last time, how little you want to take. I packed two suitcases and that was it. The whole process took about ten minutes. Oddly enough, my head was clear. It hurt, but it was clear. For the first time in years everything seemed quite simple. That panicky feeling had gone.

I climbed into the cab and told Eric to drive to London. It was half past two. As we turned into the main road I told myself: I wasn't mad at all. And I leant against the back seat.

We got quite merry in the car, and stopped in Hungerford for a cream tea. Apparently people get like this – a bit hysterical – at funerals. God knows what Eric thought as I stuffed myself with fruit cake. I was suddenly hungry. I thought of the cupboards at home, full of food; they waited for my husband. I thought how little I had known him, and wondered if other wives ever felt the same. Not the circumstances – the feelings. No wonder I had found myself talking to horses.

I'm living with my sister now. I never told her the real reason I left Ranjit. I just said I couldn't stand it, living in the sticks.

'Don't blame you,' she said. 'All those cows for company.'

'And a horse,' I replied.

'It would drive me round the bend,' she went on.

'It did.'

· *Monsters* ·

Diana

Shall I describe her? You've probably seen her yourself in the magazines, though you wouldn't know her name. Sometimes her hair is long and silky and sometimes it's been crinkled. Model girls are curiously anonymous, aren't they, except that one you see with Mick Jagger . . . you know, what's her name.

Oh yes, and in the malt whisky advertisement, when she's sitting by the fire, her hair is gently waved. In that photograph she looks quite married.

Robert hasn't married her yet; he has to wait until the winter, when the divorce comes through. What do middle-aged husbands do with their middle-aged wives? They trade them in for a younger model.

See – I haven't lost my sense of humour. Not entirely. Some people in fact – acquaintances, people

I don't know well – they even say I'm taking the whole thing remarkably well.

Jessie's not a top model, nothing like that. It's only myself who notices the photos. She's just quite successful and extremely pretty and as young as our daughters.

I'm polishing the dining-room table at the moment. Even in my lowest moments I haven't let the house go to seed. It's quite large, you see; we've brought up the girls here. I'm using lavender polish; even in my misery I can breathe, with pleasure, the smell . . . scoop it up, creamy mauve, in my cloth.

I wish I could say she was vacuous. She sometimes looks it – parted lips, spikey mascara. She isn't. I've met her, you see. At a party, at Robert's office, before any of this started. Well, I think it hadn't started by then. He runs an industrial heating firm and she had featured in one of their advertisements. She was rather amusing – I remember her mimicking her Indian TV rental man. You see, I'm not being stupidly jealous, am I? I'm being fair.

Do you want to know my secret, why I don't let the house get the better of me? I invite someone to supper. I pull myself together then, I get out the Hoover. My visitors are always complimentary, how nice everything looks, what gorgeous flowers. I think they do it to avoid a scene. And from relief

- that I've not let myself go. I haven't, of course. Not while they're in the house.

The table's all smeary now. I'm polishing it off. Robert and I bought this table – oh, years ago. We'd go round those funny little junk shops together, probably bored everybody with how little we'd paid – one realizes a lot of things later. At the time you're closed in, aren't you? A happy marriage makes one so short-sighted.

Why didn't I notice the signs, you might ask? They were obvious, I suppose – obvious to everyone else. He's always been a handsome man. He's put on a bit of weight, a bit fleshier, but it suits him. I should have realized something was up when he started growing his sideburns. And he started entertaining clients he said I'd find too boring to meet. He became more attentive to me . . . more distant but more attentive. It's so humiliating. Such a cliché, isn't it? That's been one of the more painful surprises – that Robert, who's always been so special, has acted in such a terribly predictable manner. Steph, my youngest daughter, she cried: 'How can he be so corny!'

I never let myself rip, like a fishwife. I never screamed at him. Even now, now he's gone, I don't exactly feel jealous about Jessie. Not in quite the way I expected. They call jealousy a green-eyed monster. Charming, the idea of something solid;

you can grapple with a monster. But everyone knows it's not like that . . . It's like a gas. Sometimes I feel nauseous. I have to stop and hold on to a chair, or this table, until it passes.

I'm polishing the table because Steph's coming home. It's her summer vacation, you see. They call it vacation, not holidays, at university. I'm getting the house straight. She'll be here tomorrow.

He didn't take much with him. None of this furniture. Do you know, that was one of the things that hurt most? He was so decent about that side of things. Even though, for the past few years, way before Jessie came on the scene, I'd felt that he wasn't becoming nicer, he was becoming . . . well, a bit sillier. A glassy-eyed, hectic look about him. Harder-hearted. According to Steph, it's the male menopause. I don't know whether it's a relief, that there's a word for it. I don't want the word to apply to him. Menopause, adultery . . . Words you read in magazines.

No, it wasn't Jessie who changed him. She can't give herself credit for that. She doesn't realize . . . she hasn't got the Robert I knew, and lived with, for thirty years.

No, he left nearly everything here. It did hurt. As if he were saying: my new life, it offers me better things than material possessions.

But these aren't material possessions. We've had

them too long for that. That's why it's rather painful. These marks on the table, I'm rubbing them with my cloth . . . The knife-marks the children made when they were bored, the scratches from a thousand family meals . . . Every grain, every knot so familiar to all of us . . . No! it's not just a table, of course.

Jessie

'What about white?' says Robert, and reads the label. 'Anodized aluminium.'

We're looking at tables in Habitat. It's Sunday afternoon and nearly closing time. We made love after lunch and both fell asleep afterwards.

'A bit antiseptic,' I say. 'Like an operating table.' I imagine it, shiny white in our bare white flat. We've paused, his arm tucked into mine. We feel flushed and unreal, displaced. We haven't had time for a bath. People with push-chairs and loaded carrier-bags, struggling with family paraphernalia, edge past each other muttering apologies.

'I haven't bought any food,' I say.

'We'll go out.'

'I meant to get a joint for Sunday.'

'Forget it.' He squeezes my arm and smiles down at me, his face creasing. Then he turns to inspect the table. I love his profile. It's heavy and sculptural, like an emperor's on an old coin. It's settled into its shape. The men I've known before seem just boys, shifting and unformed. He complains he's getting fat, but when I put my arms around him it's like putting them around an oak. He didn't like it once, though, when I compared him to seasoned wood.

'You mean rotten,' he said. 'Wormy.'

I tried to explain the difference but he wouldn't take it. He's sensitive about his age. He's always going on about it himself, but he doesn't like anyone else to.

'It's very modern,' I say, 'Very high tech.'

They've got some wooden ones over there, polished pine, but we've been through that. He doesn't want that sort of furniture.

'You like it, Jess?'

I nod. I don't mind. I don't care. I want him to make the decision. I just want to get it home; for us to sit at it, day after day.

We carry back the box. The table is in collapsed, kit form. I help him with it up the stairs. I'm terrified of him having a heart attack. He's fifty-three, you see. He keeps himself fit. He goes to a businessman's gym in Berkeley Square. He jogs. He is the most ardent lover. He runs his tongue over every inch of my body; he licks between my toes. Sometimes there seems a desperation in his breathing; he grips me as if I'm going to slip away. I tell him I won't.

He's assembling the table now. Apparently, back in Kensington, he kept racks of tools in the garage. Here he has so little – just some crumpled paper bags with nails and nuts in them, and a hammer with the £6.40 sticker still on it. He struggles along with these limited means.

I try to talk to him sometimes, about the past. About the house and the children. We can avoid talking about his wife if he likes. But I want to know the most ordinary, humdrum things. What they did at weekends; where the girls slept when they were little. I've seen the house but only from the street. A posh terraced place, with daffodils in the window-box. It didn't give much away.

He doesn't want to talk about it. I mustn't prod him too much. Oh, he's told me a certain amount. I don't think he deliberately keeps it from me. But he's changed his life so dramatically. We live the other side of London from his house, his girls' school, the garage that repaired his car – yesterday as he searched the yellow pages for the nearest Renault dealer, I felt such a pang for him. Most of his friends have taken Diana's side and I don't blame them. We don't see many people. We go to pubs around here – my area – and Greek restaurants and late-night shops where we buy silly expensive things to eat. We live erratically, on impulse. He enjoys that. He says it's one of the things he loves in me. 'You're so fresh,

Jess, you'll never grow old. You live each minute as it comes.' With the implied rebuke to his wife, that she didn't. But with a large house, part-time work and two children I bet I'd be exactly the same. You'd have to plan, then. I tried to say that, once, but he just smiled, he didn't really listen.

He listens to my past. Especially he questions me about my old boyfriends; he's terribly jealous. I tell him, truthfully, that he needn't be. Other people have been important to me, people he's not so interested in – my parents, my brothers. But my boyfriends weren't, not in retrospect.

He's got three of the legs on now. The table is on its back, the legs sticking into the air. We'll be sitting around it on Monday night because his daughter Stephanie's coming to dinner.

The walls are bare, except for a couple of studio shots of me that he's pinned up. I find them embarrassing. I want us to get some real pictures. We will, he says, we'll go shopping. Those photos of me, they make this place look like a studio, not a home . . . I want to see photos of his family. His wife has the albums. He has a few snapshots but I want enough to linger over. After all, he's got me. Why stick me on the walls too?

And I haven't quite got him. Oh yes, I've got this man screwing on the last leg, leaning back on his haunches, with a grunt, to rub his eye. We

make love with panic, to catch up with lost time.
There's so much catching-up to do, it seems such
a monumental task. But he won't show me where
to begin.

All those years that Diana and his daughters had
him. All those Sunday lunches, all those squabbles
about who's watching what on the TV, all those
incomprehensible family jokes . . . The eleven thousand nights, I've worked it out, that Diana shared
his bed.

He doesn't suspect me of being jealous. I don't
suppose anyone does. It's a part of my love, it
mingles with it like poisoned air. I'm jealous of
Diana, you see . . . I can admit it on the page. I
envy her the past.

'So chic,' says Stephanie, running her finger over
the white table. 'They'll be putting you in *House and
Garden*.'

We have brown paper napkins. Mine is shredded
in my lap. I'm rolling it into little pellets, like rabbit
droppings. I do like Stephanie. We've met before, in
a pub. She's spirited and sharp. It's sad that we'll
never be able to be friends.

'I like the blinds,' she says. 'Where did you
get them?'

We tell her. None of us is interested. We've
finished the duck. Shall I tell you what we've been

talking about so far? The flat. Whether we have use of the garden (we don't). Where we bought the sofa. Carefully, politely, we have talked around objects. God, we're polite. But it's easier to make a joke about the gays downstairs than approach the subject of ourselves.

Robert is waiting for her to go. Then he'll have another scotch. It's so sad, that it'll be a relief when his daughter leaves. So easy for us, once she's gone.

Stephanie has a lively face; bright eyes under a thick fringe. I can imagine her at twelve; I don't believe she's changed much. I roll the pellets. Robert will stick this through. I won't.

I clear my throat. After all, it's hardly adventurous. 'Robert says you always went to the Isle of Wight for your holidays.'

'That's right,' she says.

'I found a photo – you and Sophie sitting on a dinosaur.'

She leans forward, smiling. 'Let's have a look.'

I get up and fetch it from the drawer. It's amongst Robert's bags of nails – a buff envelope of snaps. Album rejects, odds and ends. I asked him about this one; he told me about the Isle of Wight but not enough, never enough.

Stephanie takes it, pushing back her fringe. 'That place!' For the first time her face looks open and eager. She's off her guard. 'Monster Park. We'd drag Mum and Dad there day after day. We'd make them promise, didn't we, Dad?'

Robert nods.

'You could climb all over the dinosaurs,' she laughs. 'Nobody stopped you. You could climb up their tails and slide down their necks.' She inspects the photo. 'Their backs were smooth as glass from all the children's bottoms.' She looks up. 'I remember you two hanging around, all fidgety. Children always take too long. Once I got stuck, remember?'

He nods. 'Weird place . . . Probably closed down now.' He pauses. 'Who's for coffee?'

Diana

Steph and I are going to Venice. Just for a week, for a treat. It's one of those packages. I've never been to Venice. I would never have got organized if it wasn't for Steph.

She understands why I don't care to go anywhere familiar. She doesn't want to either. When the girls were small we'd go to the coast – Devon, Kent, the Isle of Wight. That was their favourite. The Babbidge Hotel was right on the beach, perfect for children. On Saturday night they'd have a band and Robert would dance with the girls, grave and sunburnt and tall.

I think about the past every waking moment. And there's Robert, sloughing it off like an old skin. That's what people say, when they've seen him. Steph went to dinner there last week.

Steph has all these ideas. She says men can forget, they travel light because they can impregnate but not reproduce. They can move on, intact, while the women cope with the results. It's such a shock, having to apply all this theoretical stuff to Robert – all these opinions we both used to laugh at. Dear, familiar Robert – nowadays he's fitting into these ready-made slots, so very neatly.

On the way to Luton Airport we pass a hoarding. My heart quickens. It shows Jessie in a bikini. She's caramel-coloured and lounging on a raft: NIVEA BRONZING GEL.

'Imagine –' says Steph and stops.

I know: imagine those long brown legs wrapped around my husband.

'Looks monstrous from this angle,' says Steph. 'Monster legs.'

We've passed it. I do imagine that side of things – it would be foolish to pretend I didn't. But not quite as Steph supposes. As I said, the sickness catches me suddenly, off guard. After all, there's everything to make me jealous. She's beautiful, young, intelligent – yes, I forgot to tell you that. Once I found two theatre stubs in Robert's jacket pocket – corny, corny, Steph said. It was a studio theatre in Hammersmith – an experimental place. I knew Robert would never have gone there by choice. Steph, when I told her, said the tickets were the cultural equivalent of the sideburns.

No, I'm jealous of all that. Of course I am. But I've been young. I was considered good-looking. Robert and I had a marvellous sex life. I enjoy the growing beauty of my girls. People envy someone like Jessie because of their own missed opportunities, their own unfulfilment. I don't feel that.

We're driving into the long-term car park. It's a huge field, adazzle with cars. The sky is blue. No – what I envy is not quite Jessie's youth, but her newness. The way that whatever she does will be different. Different from what I did, different from what Robert has known. They have shared no past, to dull with repetition the present . . . That's what makes me feel helpless.

Jessie

We almost had our first quarrel about this holiday. You see, Robert wants to take me to Italy. He wants to go to Rome and Venice. He's never been to Venice. It does sound lovely – I do want to go. Part of our near-quarrel was that he nearly accused me of being ungracious. I tried to explain about the Isle of Wight. He thought I was mad, when we could go anywhere in the world, when we could see the Sistine Chapel together. I said, pompously, that I didn't want to discover Michelangelo, I wanted to discover him.

We made it up, of course, in bed. Actually, on the rug. I couldn't quite explain it in words – that the whole thing seems slightly unreal. We're marooned in the present, like a perpetual holiday. Cut off from the past – munching our tandoori take-aways, from their foil bags, on our shiny white table.

We settled it. We'd go to the Isle of Wight for the weekend, then next month, in August, we'll go to Italy. 'For our real holiday,' he said.

So here we are. Not in the Babbidge Hotel, of course. Somewhere more expensive, without any children at all. It's a windy, cloudy afternoon. Mellowed by an excellent lunch, including a bottle of 1971 Margaux, he's taking me to the Monster Park. I think he's humouring me.

It's not called the Monster Park, actually, it's called Slipper Chine. Chine's the word they use around here, he says, for a cliff creek. It's an incredible place. The park is very steep, almost a cliff itself, with zig-zag paths winding down through the bushes, and trees battered by the wind. Below, far down, we can see the white waves.

'Where are the dinosaurs?'

'Further down.'

We make our descent. I'm wobbling on my high heels; the wind whips my hair against my face. There are a few people about – mothers in anoraks, children shouting and running ahead. There's nobody like us. The gulls cry; parents cry out to their children.

'Did your girls run away?'

'Frequently.'

We pass large, mechanical models of nursery rhymes. Each one is set amongst the bushes, in a dusty clearing.

'Look, Robert!'

Humpty Dumpty is sitting on a plaster wall, tipping forwards and back. Creak . . . creak . . . and the leaves rustling in the wind. Humpty has thick, red lips; he leers.

Robert squeezes my arm. 'Isn't it kitsch? I love watching you – you're like a child.'

Don't look at me, look at this place. 'Was it like this?'

He nods. 'Didn't realize it was so shabby.'

Turning the corner, the wind hits us. We stagger sideways and clutch the handrail.

'Look,' he says. 'The paths have eroded since then.' Below, one path has cracked and broken away. It's fenced off, with a diversion. 'This whole place is sliding into the sea.' Far below, we can hear the breakers.

We pass a model village. The tiny church is playing music, faint in the wind. It's weird, making our way down the path. The models are either too small, like the toy church, or else monster-size, like Humpty's great peeling egg-head, creaking backwards and forwards. I think of children, running off and getting lost. I feel like Alice in Wonderland, shrinking and then swelling in this tilted landscape . . . creeping down this steep maze of paths, down the hill, down through the labyrinth of childhood.

'Tell me about it,' I say loudly. 'Which ones did the girls like best?'

He says something. The wind whips his words away.

'What?' I shout. There's a gale blowing up.

'I've forgotten!' he shouts back.

We come across a pokerwork sign: DINOSAURS THIS WAY. We walk down the path.

'Oh look!'

A giant head is gazing down at us. It has glass eyes. Its huge body stands amongst the bushes. DIPLODOCUS, says the label.

'They've had to prop him up.' Robert points to the scaffolding wedged against the creature's flanks. It has become very cold. A fine mist has drifted in from the sea and most of the other people seem to have gone.

'We should be getting back!' shouts Robert. 'You must be freezing in that dress.'

'Just a bit more!'

He replies but the wind blows the words away. We walk on down. Through the bushes other monsters are revealed – horned beasts standing in the clearings, looking startlingly real. TYRANNOSAURUS REX is reared up on his hind legs.

'I can't see the one in the photo!' I shout. 'Which is it?'

'How can I remember?'

The path is steep; I hold on to the rail. 'It looks like that one.'

It's a monster lizard, low on the ground, with a thick tail. I pull Robert to a stop. The mist is thicker here.

'Isn't this it?'

'I don't know!' he shouts in my ear.

'You're not interested!' My voice rises shrilly. 'I'm more interested in your family than you are!'

He turns away. I can't hear.

'What?'

He turns back. 'Don't you tell me what my feelings are!'

'Have you got any? Sometimes I wonder. You seem so numb.'

He lets go my arm. 'Listen to me, Jessica. Just listen, will you? What do you want me to say? That

I had a miserable life until you came along? That's
what you want?'

'No!'

'Because if you do, I can't oblige. Understand?'

'But –'

He suddenly shouts: 'If you must know, it was
bloody marvellous with the girls! Oh yes, ups and
downs, but bloody marvellous.'

'But I'm glad. I don't want you to have been
miserable.'

'I was also rather happy with my wife. For a good
many years, anyway –'

'I know!'

He turns; the wind whips away his words.

'What?' I screech.

He turns back. 'I always thought you were so
free,' he yells. 'So unfettered.'

'I don't want to fetter you, I –'

'Come on, it's freezing.' He's breathing heavily;
his face is flushed. He turns and starts walking up
the path.

'I don't!' I'm clattering along behind. 'I love you
. . . I can't help . . .'

He's striding up the path. I'm breathless. Huge
bodies appear out of the mist. I'm shocked by the
bitterness I've uncovered in him. I'm also shocked
by my own greed. Worse is my jealousy of his
wife who has had so much, even a thousand more

quarrels than I could possibly have. These monster feelings, we've kept them well hidden.

'Wait!' I call.

He can't hear me. He's striding ahead. I stumble after him.

'Robert!' I yell. For the first time in five months he's ignoring me. I can't catch my breath.

He's stopped at a bench. He sits down, suddenly.

'Darling!' I'm hurrying up to him. It's all right. He's stopped for me.

I get nearer. He's leaning forward, looking thoughtfully at the path. We didn't mean it, either of us. We won't talk about it again. I sit down. He's gazing at the tarmac; I put my arm around him.

I begin: 'Robert, I didn't mean . . .'

He's whispering something. I stop. There's something wrong.

'Robert?'

He's not looking at the path. I realize now that his eyes are clenched shut. I lean nearer.

He whispers: 'Chest.'

Diana

I met her at the funeral. We happened to come out of the porch together, and said a few words.

Do you know, there was a photo of us two, rather blurred, in the local paper. Jessie and myself.

Caught for a moment together. We'll never meet again.

I put it in the album. I need to keep anything connected with him. Once or twice I've looked at it. After all, she was a part of Robert. I don't feel any emotion about her, except pity. She blames herself for his heart attack, you see. I never dared ask her how it happened, in case she'd have to say they were making love.

I feel pity too, for another reason. We both loved him. But who has the most, now, to remember?

I had thirty years.

· *Snake Girl* ·

*E*veryone liked Johnnie. Always a smile, and first with the drinks at the Sind Club bar. Last to leave, too, but then he lived alone and where else would he go?

He would horse around with the kids, as well, at the Sind Club pool. His jokes were sometimes of a robust nature, for down in the bazaar he knew a supplier of plastic masks. Mothers liked him because they could dreamily give themselves up to the sun. Their children called him uncle and chased him, whooping, through the verandas. Turbaned bearers stepped aside. 'He's never grown up,' parents said, as they sipped lime sodas under the dusty palms. 'He's a child himself.' Sometimes, when they were posted elsewhere, as they inevitably were, they told their children to send him a postcard. Sometimes they remembered.

Nobody knew when he had come to Pakistan. He was simply one of the fixtures and fittings: a

lean man in a beige bush-jacket, who could tell a
newcomer where to buy the best Beluchi carpets
and who knew all the reels for Burns Night. This
happened once a year at the Consulate; he was
paired off with career secretaries of uncertain age
and American divorcees who chomped on menthol
cigarettes and sometimes, unsuccessfully, asked him
back to their place. There was Johnnie, blurred in
the corner of a hundred snapshots, caught for ever in
a lost episode in people's lives – before Washington,
before London again, before their divorce and the
dispersal of their growing children. 'Isn't that him?'
they'd point. Fixed, his face, eager to please in the
blinking rabbit glare. Passingly, they felt curious.

He had an ageless, leathery look, from decades
in the sun. He was a bachelor, and one of those
innocents who survive surprisingly well in a devious
country. How old was he: forty-five? fifty-five? He
wasn't secretive; it's just that if one does not offer
information there are others more ready with their
own, busy selves. Johnnie was a spectator, and one
of that rare breed: a truly modest man.

He was British; a pilot with P I A. Few people
knew his real name; he had been nicknamed Johnnie
Walker on account of the whisky which in those days
cost Rs 300 per bottle on the black market. At his
shindigs there was always plenty of that, what with
his airline connections and his legendary generosity.

And plenty of homemade beer, which he brewed
in buckets and called hooch. His cronies slapped
him on the back; the Pakistani ones called him
'old chap'.

Why had he never married? Jokingly he said that
he'd missed his connection and the flight was never
called. Besides, he was always somewhere else –
Frankfurt one day, New York the next, standing
the crew a drink in the bar of some intercontinental
hotel. He wore the glazed bonhomie, the laun-
dered pleasantness, of the permanently jetlagged.
He returned with perfume for the plainest girls at
the British Consulate, who thanked him wistfully. If
people paused to wonder, they decided that his true
love was planes – after all, the flight deck of a DC10
was simpler than any woman. And what could beat
the romance of flying – lights blipping, that vast blue
space above, arriving only to depart, the sweet angst
of loss flavouring every encounter? He adored his
job, that was plain; just look at his flat.

You had to duck to get into the living-room.
This was due to the model planes suspended from
the ceiling. Hurricanes, Spitfires, Mosquitoes –
civilian and military aircraft, revolving slowly in
the breeze from the fan. Otherwise his flat had a
transitory air. It was situated on the new beach
road outside the city: Route 43, that so far led
nowhere. Apartment blocks had been built along

it but in those days, the mid-seventies, they had not yet been completed; most were still concrete cells with electrical wires knotted from the ceiling, and a view of the sea. The parking spaces in front were edged with oil drums, from each of which drooped a bougainvillea bush.

Hot wind blew, sand against concrete. Behind the flats stretched the grey desert.

'One day,' he joked, 'this'll be the Third World's answer to Malibu Beach.' People asked him if he felt lonely, living with the few other pioneers in Phase One, and he replied: 'Me, lonely? With the best view in Pakistan?'

He said the sun setting over the Arabian Ocean was beautiful, but most sundowns he was to be found at the Sind Club bar.

Then in 1975, to everybody's surprise, Johnnie married. Gossip buzzed in the Sind Club bar; after all, there was little else to gossip about. 'Young enough to be his daughter.' A nudge and a wink. 'He's landed on his feet,' said Mr Bashir from Cameron Chemicals. 'Has he?' asked Kenneth Trimmer from Grindlays Bank. What did she see in him, and he in her? She was a small, gaudy Pakistani girl, seemingly sprung from nowhere. But then Karachi was used to arrivals and departures; the airport road was the busiest in the city.

Another nudge and wink. Above, the ceiling fans creaked. Along the walls, bearers stood like waxworks. Beyond, the tree frogs whirred; beyond them, beyond the beach route and the apartment blocks, the hot wind blew in from the sea.

She had sprung from nowhere. At least, she was new to him. Music thudded from his lounge, where his guests gyrated under the swaying aircraft. There she was in his kitchen, buttering a slice of bread.

'You look starving,' he said.

She gazed up at him. She had large black eyes and shiny lipstick. 'Someone said there was smoked salmon.'

'All gone.' A plate lay there, scattered with lime wedges. 'I brought it back from London.'

'You're the pilot then?'

He nodded. He wanted to feed her up. He opened the fridge but by this stage in the evening everything had been eaten.

'Jam?' he asked. She nodded. She was wearing jeans and a yellow T-shirt with spangles on it. Despite the make-up, and the indolent way she pushed her hair behind her ear, she looked so young. She ate greedily.

Her name was Aisha and she had come with Farooq and his crowd – young bloods who drove their Daddies' cars and went to the Excelsior Hot

Spot. They knew the location of parties by a kind of radar.

And Aisha disappeared with them, with honking horns from down below and a slewing of tyres. Johnnie was left amongst the ashtrays, and when he moved to the window there was nothing but a huge moon silvering the sea. A string of street lights led to Karachi. He thought of flying, of cities laid out below like winking puzzles that sometimes made sense; he thought of his own back which was starting to ache whenever he leant over. He picked up a glass and straightened with a grunt.

The next flight to London he bought back a packet of smoked salmon and put it in his fridge. And a few days later he found her.

It was in downtown Karachi. Through a haze of exhaust smoke he spotted her outside the Reptile Emporium. Air crews bought shoes and handbags there; she was looking at the window display. He wanted to buy up the shop; he wanted to please her.

Nearby, a pavement kiosk sold cigarettes. But also, for those who knew, copies of *Vogue* and *Penthouse* could be produced from under the counter. He asked to see the selection. Inspired, he knew just what she wanted: a glossy copy of the Harrods Christmas catalogue.

They sat in an open-air café behind the Metropole Hotel. Against the white glare of the sky a sign stuttered for 7-*Up*. She drank through a straw and pointed to photos of ostrich-trimmed nightgowns. 'Ooh,' she gasped.

The next page was a festive table, laden with food; it glowed in the candlelight. 'Look,' she pointed. There were two brushed children and their parents gathered around a pile of presents, which were wrapped in ribbon. Behind them an olde-worlde window was speckled with snow.

'I want to go to England,' she sighed.

He smiled. 'It doesn't really look like that.'

Two street urchins came into the café and held out their hands. 'Baksheesh!' they demanded. She shooshed them away. Johnnie, however, gave them Rs 5 each – far too much. They sniggered and ran off. Today he felt foolish; he felt young.

Two months later they were married. He had never been so happy. Aisha sat on his knee and he told her about Singapore and Sydney. Her eyes widened; she stroked his cheek.

She liked jokes, too. One evening she put on a small black moustache.

Startled, he asked: 'What's this – Hitler?'

She knew nothing of the Second World War. She replied: 'Look, I'm Charlie Chaplin?' She loved the movies and could see the same ones again and again.

In their high apartment they gazed out at the sea; they ate smoked salmon and Bentinck's Bittermints. Some other windows were lit now, and sweetmeat sellers had set up their stalls on the sand. With his wife on his knee, his flat became his home. He was no longer seen at the Sind Club; she thought it fuddy-duddy, with its shrouded billiards tables and relics of the Raj. She preferred the beach. Young men from the city drove out nowadays, their car boots clanking with crates of Bubble-Up and their radios blaring. The place was being developed into a seaside resort of a minor nature. Fairy lights had been strung around a chicken-tikka café. Bold couples parked their cars and necked.

His own bearer had left, disapproving of this plump young woman who had bewitched his master. Neither Johnnie nor Aisha could cook, so the two of them went down to the beach café and sat on mismatched plastic chairs. They drank sweet tea while car radios played film music and the sea sighed, vastly. Young men ogled her; she shouted back at them – Urdu oaths which even Johnnie, an old trooper, couldn't understand.

Once he asked her about Farooq, who had brought her to the party, but she just shrugged. Farooq's family was in favour with the Bhutto government and involved in developing the beach; they had landed the contract to build a casino. One evening he and his friends arrived and dragged Aisha, squealing, to the water's edge. They sauntered back, their cigarettes glowing in the dark. Later she showed Johnnie the mark on her wrist where Farooq had gripped her. He was angry, but she shrugged. 'Stupid Rooqi,' she said, with one of her baffling smiles. He felt pain, first for her and then for himself.

'In England she'd be called a scrubber,' said Shirley Trimmer, 'but I like her.'

They were driving home from a Sind Club dinnerdance. 'Not top drawer,' said her husband Kenneth. 'But then, if one thinks of it, neither is he.'

It had been a stifling evening – an elderly band playing Frank Ifield tunes; polite wives in saris. She glanced at Kenneth. He was putting on weight. He had never been as pompous as this in England, but then in England he had never been a sahib.

She sighed and looked out of the window. Something was caught in the glare of the headlights. It was a camel, bedecked with beads. It turned its head slowly, like a puppet. She felt a rush of pleasure – the first, and last, of the evening.

Like her husband, Aisha was a lost soul, an orphan. Sometimes she talked about the past, but it was always the far past, when she was a child. Her father had been the assistant clerk of an irrigation scheme up in the north, in the Punjab. She talked about the ditches filled with brown water, the banks moulded like putty. She didn't use those words, but Johnnie pictured it.

He stroked her hair as she sat, curled in the armchair, and told him how she had adored her father and how she had followed him along the canals. He didn't know she was following him; he would have been angry. One day she lost him; she remembered looking down and seeing the water moving with snakes. Long, shiny snakes, they had coiled and knotted themselves in the water which was as warm as soup.

Johnnie tilted her face towards him; her jaws worked as she chewed on her gum. He was filled with such tenderness that his limbs felt boneless.

'My serpent of old Nile,' he said.

'Pardon?'

'William Shakespeare,' he replied.

She smiled and turned the page of *Movie Secrets*.

'My snake girl,' he said.

She shivered. 'Ugh! I hate snakes.'

Kenneth and Shirley Trimmer came out of the Reptile Emporium. It was May, and the suffocating weather just beginning.

She was carrying her new snakeskin shoes. 'You shouldn't have bargained!' she hissed.

'They respect you for it,' he replied. 'You should understand by now.'

'Don't be condescending.'

'My dear, they're all on the fiddle.'

Only recently had he started calling her dear. She looked at him coolly. The subcontinent was turning him into the housemaster of a minor prep school. She should have suspected it.

Ahead she spotted Johnnie and his wife; Aisha wore luminous pink shalwar-kamize pyjamas and red high heels. She clung to his arm as they hailed a taxi.

'Don't they look happy,' Shirley said.

'Who?' He was not an observant man. She pointed them out. He said: 'Obvious, isn't it. She's looking for a father and he's looking for a daughter. Won't last.'

There were damp semi-circles under his arms. She turned away and thought: But will we?

When Johnnie flew, he flew for his wife. Planes simply became vehicles to shorten the distance until he held her again. In foreign hotels his heart ached. He only found peace browsing in the gift arcades.

Sometimes he managed to get through on the phone – the lines to Pakistan were erratic – but often there was no reply. On his return he never asked her about this; he was too old to want to know the answer.

He returned, laden with gifts. Once, when he came home from a long haul and the phone had never answered, she gave him a present.

He unwrapped the box. It was a Mark V Spitfire, ready-assembled. In fact he had one already, suspended near the kitchen door, but though she had tried to learn the difference between his planes she had never succeeded.

'Do you like it?' she asked. 'There is a toy-wallah in Bohri Bazaar. I told him to make it for you.'

Deeply moved, he hugged her. How could he explain that the fun was in doing-it-yourself? For her, the fun was not-doing-it-yourself.

She didn't understand him. But what did that matter when in some obscure way, he could never find the words for it, they were two of a kind? He loved her all the more.

One day Shirley bumped into Aisha in Bohri Bazaar, the main bazaar of the city. Along the alleys, saris hung like flags; village women shuffled past, shrouded in bourquas like grubby sheets; a legless beggar sat on his trolley and the air smelt of incense.

'I'm going to London soon,' said Aisha. 'I'm going to Oxford Street.'

Shirley grimaced. 'It's awful. Tacky and crowded.'

Aisha gestured around. 'But this is dirty and crowded.'

'No,' smiled Shirley. 'This is romantic.'

Aisha wrinkled her nose. 'You English people, you must be mad.'

He wanted to show her the world; on the other hand he wanted to keep her safe. For the first time in his career he thought of hijackers and metal fatigue. He blamed this for his reluctance.

But how her eyes would widen at the England she desired so fiercely: acres of separates at Marks & Spencers; fairy lights not over a tikka café but looped high around Harrods; clean, moneyed streets.

He himself had lived abroad for so many years that by now this was his England too. He too saw it from an air-conditioned transit bus; he had become an outsider. London was where you bought gift-wrapped jars of marmalade and where people still sometimes said *I'm sorry*. If you move from one scentless hotel room to another, cities blur. They become a fast flip of picture postcards and a memento, at the bottom of your suitcase, you forgot you bought.

He fixed them a holiday in London, for two weeks in October. He booked her a direct flight; he himself would be arriving from New York. They planned to meet in the hotel. 'It's our honeymoon,' he told her, though they had been married a year. He booked a room overlooking Hyde Park, so that when she opened the window, for the first time in her life she would smell autumn. He pictured the two of them, laden with carrier-bags, walking beside the lake and kicking the leaves. He hadn't kicked leaves since he was a boy, and seldom then. He had been raised in an orphanage. He hadn't kept this a secret; it was just that nobody asked. It was his wife who fifty years later was giving him back his childhood. For this he would give her the world, which he had crossed so many times alone. If not the world, at least he would give her London.

He was leaving two days earlier than Aisha. He hugged her. Ridiculously, his stomach churned. He had never before suffered from flight-nerves.

'Look after yourself,' he murmured. He pressed her glossy head to his chest. She gripped him. 'Fly to me safely.'

'You always say it's the safest way to travel.'

'But you're different,' he said.

'Why?'

'You're precious.'

When he left, a gust of wind blew through the apartment. Doors slammed; the planes rocked.

All that evening a gale blew in from the sea. Sand dimmed the sunset; drifts half-buried the café chairs. Down in the city, dust swirled.

Shirley, emerging from a business function at the Metropole Hotel, saw Aisha climbing out of a Mercedes. Giggling, she was smoothing down her loose lurex slacks which billowed in the wind. Another girl followed her, and three Pakistani men. Cigarettes glowing, the men propelled the girls downstairs into the Excelsior Hot Spot.

Shirley climbed into her own car and sat next to her husband. She thought: Aisha is an innocent. Not as nice as Johnnie, but an innocent too.

Now why did she think that? The words jostled in her head; a puzzle she hadn't the will to work out. Let them get on with it, she thought recklessly. Tonight she was tipsy. She had drunk a great deal of Rs 300-a-bottle imported gin.

Perhaps, when he returned, Johnnie would hold one of his shindigs. Ah, she remembered, but by then she and Kenneth would be back in London; his contract finished at the end of the month.

At that moment, as they drove through the dusty street, palm trees swaying in the headlights, Kenneth clearing his throat beside her – at that moment, with the crystal clarity that alcohol can bring, she knew that once she returned to England she would leave him.

In the subcontinent, the most beautiful times are dawn and dusk. Johnnie had often remarked upon this. The sky was pearly-pink as Aisha sat in the car with Farooq. The storm had passed; the sea glinted, swelling like oil. It was the early morning. Across the world, across time zones, her husband slept. Or maybe he was eating lunch. Who knew? Painfully, she wished she did.

Farooq kissed her forehead. 'You'll adore Yasmin,' he said. 'She's a terrific girl.' He withdrew his hand from inside her blouse and reached into the back seat. 'Remember, Thursday morning. Where?'

'The Kardomah Café,' she repeated.

'And where is that?'

She closed her eyes. 'In Oxford Street.'

'Where in Oxford Street?'

She paused, and said dreamily: 'Opposite Marks & Spencers.'

He passed her the parcel. It was a box, wrapped in ribbon. 'No peeking,' he said. There were drops of perspiration on his forehead.

'It's her birthday present?' she asked again.

He nodded. 'Snakeskin shoes from the Reptile Emporium.'

'Snakeskin.' She shivered.

'My sister adores it, and it's frightfully expensive in London.'

She closed her eyes again. 'I'm going to Harrods and Marks & Spencers and Selfridges –'

'Yasmin'll take you. She knows simply everybody and everywhere. Shops, nightclubs, you name it.'

'Johnnie and I don't know anybody.'

'Trust her. Have a sooper-dooper time.' He took her arm and folded it around the parcel. 'And don't forget this, will you?' He kissed her lightly. 'Sweetie.'

She flew overnight. Below lay the glittering grids of cities; around and above, black space. Whimpering, she pressed the airline pillow to her cheek; she felt rigid with fear. She had never flown. Surely the plane would fall? Surely Johnnie would not be there?

The cabin bucked. Everyone else slept blamelessly. 'Just a little turbulence,' the stewardess told her, as Aisha gripped her hand.

She clenched her eyes shut. She tried to rub out the thought of Farooq's hand between her thighs. She knew she was wicked, and that she would be punished.

They didn't believe her. Who would believe an

overdressed Pakistani girl, no better than a tart, who reeked of cheap perfume and scratched the customs officer with her crimson fingernails? She yelled that the box wasn't hers, it was given to her by a friend. Who? Called Farooq. Farooq who? She didn't know. She had never known his surname but he was a good friend, his father knew the President. What sort of friend is that, they asked, that you don't know his surname? Where did he live? She didn't know.

The packet was laid out on the table: small, white and smug. There were now four officers in the room. She struggled; the policewoman held her down.

She screeched: 'He said they were shoes!'

'Yes, dear.'

'Snakeskin shoes!'

By now she was hysterical. She twisted in the policewoman's arms; she spat like a cat. She was pregnant, she yelled, she was ill, she wanted her father, he was a very important person, he was a personal friend of President Bhutto. She started swearing in Urdu. They frowned, looking at the flimsy walls; people would think they were beating her up.

The mascara ran down her cheeks, her voice rose higher. She wanted her husband, he was very important too, he knew everybody, all the places to go. Her mother was sick, her mother was dying, she had to get out. Where did her mother live? they asked.

She tried to struggle free. 'At Harrods!' she shouted.

An hour later Johnnie arrived, breathlessly. They were trying to take a statement from her; she had jammed shut the lavatory door and was yelling for her husband. He heard her shrill voice; his heart shifted.

It only took him a moment to realize what had happened. It all made the most painful sense, but he didn't want to think about it. He only knew that she meant everything to him and that the world was senseless without her. He stood, swaying with fatigue, staring at the creamy walls.

For cocaine smuggling she would get at least a year in prison, his darling wife. Or maybe they would deport her and she could never visit Britain again, all her life.

He heard her voice approaching as she was dragged out of the toilets. She sounded coarse as a fishwife; he had learnt some of the oaths by now, but he would always love her.

He cleared his throat and addressed the police officer.

'I did it,' he said. 'I put it in her suitcase.'

He was sentenced to a year. Remarks were made

about a man in his position, a senior pilot, and how he had abused a job that demanded the utmost trust and integrity. Regrets were expressed that a man with such a distinguished wartime record could end his career on such a note of disgrace. More abominably, that in doing so he had tried to corrupt a simple-minded girl who was young enough to be his daughter. What were the British coming to?

In his absence the Sind Club members learnt more about Johnnie than they had ever learnt when he was there. His real name was James and he had been decorated for bravery in action during the war; he had been a fighter pilot, flying Hurricanes, and one had been shot in flames from beneath him. As a child he had lived in institutions; once grown up, he had restlessly moved from place to place, living at one time in Australia and then Canada. Finally in the forties he had moved to Karachi. Until now his record had been blameless.

'Well, well, so he's a crook,' said Mr Khan, who that morning had slipped Rs 30,000 to his good friend Habibsahib at the Port Authority, to facilitate the importation of some air-conditioners in which he himself happened to have an interest. 'I always said there was something odd about this chap Johnnie, he was so nice to everybody.'

*   *   *

It is the next summer, 1977. At the far end of the beach route the casino remains uncompleted. It is simply a concrete shell, a monument to the corrupt Bhutto regime which is now ending. There will soon be bloodshed. In July Bhutto himself will be thrown into prison and some months later executed. Martial government and strict Islamic law will be imposed on the country; gambling will be forbidden and drink no longer available even on the black market. No more shindigs. This will be a New Era of Purity.

Farooq and his family, having Bhutto connections, are now out of favour and have fled the country. They were last heard of living in Knightsbridge.

Aisha had unwittingly told the truth, the previous October; she was indeed pregnant. This summer she gives birth to a boy. The baby's skin is surprisingly dark but this is never mentioned either by herself or by Johnnie. Neither wishes to. He dotes on the child.

He is no longer employed by PIA, but then he says that he always wanted early retirement. Flying has lost its importance; he prefers to be at home sweet home. Phase One is now finished and a small bazaar has sprung up between the apartment blocks. Aisha shops there, ordering aubergines and onions to be piled into her increasingly frail Harrods carrier-bag. When she passes the cars, parked facing the beach, she rolls her eyes at the young men. Nothing will change her, but Johnnie has always known that.

One evening, unused to the heat, June and David drive out to the beach. They are new arrivals; he is Kenneth's successor at Grindlays Bank. To mark his status as sahib and branch manager he is trying to grow a small moustache.

There is a café on the beach. Johnnie and Aisha are sitting there. Johnnie holds the baby in one arm while with the other he passes a model aeroplane to and fro above its head. He makes aeroplane sounds.

David turns to his wife. 'Isn't that the chap who went to prison?' he asks. 'Unlikely-looking couple, aren't they?'

June sighs, but so softly her husband doesn't hear. She watches them for a moment, then she says: 'They do look happy.'

· *Vacant Possession* ·

Some people call us cynics. Us, being estate agents. With a chortle they quote our advertisements: 'STUDIO FLAT,' they read. 'You mean a bedsit. EASILY MAINTAINED GARDEN. You mean four square yards of concrete.'

I'm not a cynic. In fact, I'm the opposite. I'm a romantic. I see the possibilities in the meanest property. I don't just see it; I believe it. For instance, I don't tell myself that a garden is surrounded by buildings, I tell myself it's secluded. If a flat overlooks Tesco's loading bay I tell myself it's convenient for the shops.

And to my surprise it works. If you're blind to the disadvantages, you pull other people along with you in the warm slipstream of your vision. Next time you're in the Fulham area, drive around and have a look at all those boards up saying FOR SALE: PREWITT, CUDLIP & LITTLE. Cudlip's me.

Oh yes, this optimism has got me a long way

professionally. In my private life, however, it's been a different matter. Only the most foolish of romantics, the blindest of fools, would believe that a married man, working for the Department of the Environment, with three teenage children, would ever leave his wife.

Nigel was going to, of course. But not quite yet, because Vicky was doing her O-levels and he'd never be able to forgive himself if she failed. Because his wife was depressed after her hysterectomy and he couldn't bear to upset her just yet. Because, because.

They had gone on for four years, these becauses, and meanwhile I'd see him once a week or once a fortnight, when I was known as a conference in Southampton or a meeting in Hull. I'd been every major town in the British Isles. Once, for a couple of days, I was actually a summit meeting in Brussels.

Work is easy, isn't it, compared to everything else. I would sit in my beige office with its warbling phones and its window display of dream houses which I passed from one stranger to another. I would drive around in my shiny Metro, making valuations on the properties of Fash Fulham. I worked out percentages on my calculator; how cool those numbers were, how simple the soft bleeps of my sums.

If you want to know what sort of properties we handle, then Marcus Tanner's house was typical.

I'd already acted for several clients in Foster Road, a street once occupied by the humble. A few still remained, with their net curtains and polished front steps, the crysanths carefully staked in the gardens. But they were a vanishing species, outnumbered by the middle classes who knocked through their ground floors, called to each other in fruity, confident voices and filled up the street with their double-parked Renaults.

It was a morning in May that I went to Marcus Tanner's house to make a valuation. I guessed the reason for selling when I saw that the tubs on each side of the front door were choked with weeds. After six years in the house trade, I can recognize a divorce.

'Think you can shift it?' he asked. 'Quick?'

I nodded. 'No problem. These houses always sell. They're so sweet.'

'You mean small.'

'I mean sweet. Bijou. Perfect for –' I stopped. He sighed. 'It was.'

Blushing, I gazed around the lounge. It was a typical late-seventies job – open plan; William Morris wallpaper; corduroy sofa; pub mirrors; Maggie Thatcher candle.

I paced the carpet. 'Hold this, will you please?' I gave him one end of the tape measure. 'Immaculate through-lounge,' I murmured.

'Immaculate?' He raised his eyebrows. 'Looks a bit battle-scarred to me.'

I ignored him. 'Period features retained.'

'You mean these grotty old cupboards?'

I looked at him. 'You want to sell this house or not?'

He grinned. 'For a moment I thought you were a romantic.'

'Oh no. I'm a businesswoman.'

We went into the kitchen. 'Compact,' I muttered.

'You mean it's a cupboard. Hey, don't lean on those shelves, I put them up.'

'Everything within reach,' I said, measuring it.

'Shall I tell you about the dry rot?'

'No.'

We went outside.

'Even you can't pretend this is a garden,' he said.

'No, but it's a suntrap patio.'

He paused, picking a weed out of the wall. 'I'll miss this place. It's full of single-parent actresses. On Sundays you hear them learning their lines. And then there's the Sloane girls who've been bought their houses by Daddy. On summer evenings you can hear the pop of Waitrose hock bottles and the rustle of After Eights.'

'Now who's sounding romantic.'

'No. Just over-sexed.'

We went inside.

'It's an up-and-coming area,' I said.

He sighed, and inspected himself in the passage mirror. 'Look at these period features.'

He looked all right to me: a big chap, I would say in his early forties. Big but not fat – beefy. A lived-in, humorous face. I seem to have a weakness for older men. He wore a tired-looking jacket and corduroy trousers.

We went upstairs. Halfway up, I paused and looked out on to the extension roof. There was a flowerpot there, with shrivelled foliage.

He asked. 'What are you writing?'

'Roof terrace.'

We went into the bedroom. Being an estate agent, I've become an expert on divorces: weeds in the tubs, cracks in the walls. To me, the outsider on the inside, entering their lives at a moment of stress, they divide into two sorts. The ones who say nothing (men) and the ones who say too much (women). But Mr Tanner, unlike most men, wanted to tell me about it.

'Spacious fitted cupboards throughout,' I murmured, writing it down.

He opened one. It was full of dresses. 'She's coming for them tomorrow. It'll look even more spacious then.'

'What about the carpet?'

'Oh, get rid of the lot.' He paused, gazing at the bed. A cat lay curled there, its fur lit by sunlight. 'Looks peaceful, doesn't she?'

I gazed at the cat nestling on the daisy-patterned duvet, and nodded.

'She left me for her T'ai Chi instructor.'

'What?'

'Chinese martial arts.' He shut the cupboard with a snap. 'Spiritual self-defence. She was taking classes.'

'So he's Chinese?'

'No. From Tufnell Park. Between you and me, a bit of a wanker. But then I'm biased.'

There was a moment's silence. We stood in the bedroom, listening to the far strains of Radio One coming from the opposite house, which was being done up. No doubt another couple was moving in there, full of hope. I thought of the wheel of fortune, turning. Couples rising, and the casualties fallen by the wayside. Him, for instance; and me. I was not becoming a cynic.

'Enough maudlin talk,' he said. 'How much can we ask?'

'Sixty-eight,' I said briskly. 'Are you open to offers?'

He grinned again. 'Depends who's offering.'

He worked at the BBC, so he was out all day. Over

the next week I showed prospective buyers around the house. After all these years I still feel intrusive, letting myself in through somebody else's front door. Particularly when that person lives alone; their solitary possessions seem vulnerable when exposed to strangers.

I showed round young couples who lingered, arm-in-arm. 'Lime-green!' said one girl. 'What a ghastly colour for a bathroom.' In the kitchen, an officious young man prodded the shelves. 'What a wally job. Wonder who put these up.'

I felt prickly. I told myself it was simple jealousy. These people were couples, and they were actually buying a house. They would walk down a street together, arm-in-arm, in broad daylight.

I looked at the bowl of half-eaten Weetabix and wondered if Marcus Tanner always ate his breakfast standing up in the kitchen. I wondered how he passed his evenings. In the lounge one day, while the floorboards above creaked with yet another couple, I found an open *Time Out* next to the phone; various cinemas had been underlined. He'd been doodling in the margins, and he'd drawn specs on Helen Mirren.

The cat, disturbed from her bed, came downstairs and rubbed herself against my legs. I fetched a tin and fed her. Even though I didn't know her name, I felt at home then.

It was Thursday. That evening I was expecting a visit from Nigel. We were going to a suburban cinema, where we couldn't be spotted, to watch *Gandhi*. I realized how I had been changing recently. Once I would have resented *Gandhi* because it was three hours long and that meant three hours missed when I could have had Nigel to myself, in bed. Now I just wanted to see the film. I thought: I'm curing myself. The cure is working.

But in the end it was immaterial because he phoned up with his call-box whisper, and said he couldn't come because his son had been sent down from Oxford for possessing cannabis and they had to have a family confrontation.

So I went to *Gandhi* alone, at my local. At least I didn't have to travel all the way to Orpington. The next morning he sent me a bunch of roses in apology. I shoved them into the swing-bin, jamming down their heads in a crackle of cellophane.

When I went to Marcus Tanner's house that morning there were two empty wine glasses on the table. In the kitchen I found two coffee cups; it wasn't his usual Nescafé, he'd made proper coffee in his cafetière. Two breakfast plates, with toast crumbs. Irritably I thought: what a mess. How's he going to sell his house if he leaves it like this?

I was called upstairs then. The people wanted to know if the blinds went with the house. I answered them, gazing at the bed. Beside it were two glasses and a half-empty bottle of Calvados. And his Maggie Thatcher candle, burnt down to a pair of sloping blue shoulders. She must have been important, for him to have burnt his candle.

'Pardon?'

'I said,' the man repeated, 'is the seller open to offers?'

I replied: 'Apparently.'

A week later an offer was made, and accepted. I spoke to Marcus Tanner on the phone.

'Come out and celebrate,' he said. 'Say you will.'

'You only got sixty-two thousand.'

'I knew you were an optimist. A romantic.'

'I'm a businesswoman.'

'Forget business,' he said. 'I'll give you a meal.'

He took me to a Fulham Road bistro. The evening got off on the wrong foot when one of the waiters looked at me, then winked at him.

'I see you're known here,' I said.

'Oh yes,' he said blandly. He was wearing a red shirt and a bright blue tie. In the candle-light he looked caddish; a divorced man on the loose.

'Have you found somewhere else?' I asked.

'I'm looking. A flat in Barnes, I thought. Lots of BBC people in Barnes.'

'Lots of actresses.'

'Lots.'

I looked down and ordered veal, the most expensive thing on the menu.

The wine arrived. He said: 'Glad I didn't get Prewitt or Little.'

'Watch it. They're my partners.'

'But they're not as pretty.'

'They're blokes.'

'I don't go for blokes.'

'I've gathered that.'

He laughed. My neck heated up. I sipped my wine and thought of the breakfast coffee cups, and despised myself. Why shouldn't the chap enjoy himself?

I thought: catch me becoming another melted portion of Maggie Thatcher. Blushing harder, I thought: What on earth am I thinking?

We ate our antipasto. For a while it went all right. He wanted to know how I'd got into the business and I told him about my flat, and my brother's awful wife who hoovered under his lifted feet, and what I'd thought of *Gandhi*. I hadn't talked so much for ages; he made the words come into my head. I found I was entertaining even myself.

Then he said: 'Who is he?'

'Who's who?'

'There must be some lucky bloke, somewhere.'

I paused. 'Well . . .' I speared an anchovy.

'Go on. I've been longing to ask.'

'It's all . . . well, rather difficult.'

'Ah. That sort of difficult.'

I glanced up sharply. 'No!'

'Jesus,' he said. 'What a waste.'

'It's not!'

'How long has it been going on? Do you mind me asking?'

'Yes. No.' I ate a green bean. 'Four years.'

'Four? That's appalling.'

'It's not appalling. It's . . . difficult.'

'So you sit by the phone, and when it rings there's that pip-pip-pip?'

I said coldly: 'You're obviously speaking from experience.'

He ignored me. 'And all weekend you wash your hair, and hear the hours ticking away, and watch the families in the park –'

'Marcus, shut up!'

'And he keeps promising he'll leave her, and sometimes he even breaks down and cries –'

'Look –'

'– a grown man, and that makes you feel even worse.'

'Marcus –'

'And so you throw yourself into your work, and sublimate –'

Furious, I shouted: 'What a stupid, sexist remark! You wouldn't say that if I were a man.'

'I wouldn't feel like this if you were a man.'

I pushed an olive around my plate. 'It's none of your business.'

We fell silent. After a while we started talking politely. It was Wimbledon fortnight and we discussed McEnroe, but the zest had gone.

Outside he offered to drive me home but I said I would rather walk. I thanked him for the dinner.

He took my hand. 'Sorry.'

'It doesn't matter.'

'It does.' Lorries rattled past. He was gazing at me, frowning. 'Four years is a long time. I just feel . . . you ought to be more honest with yourself. Not such a romantic.' He paused. 'You should face up to reality.'

'I do!'

He smiled. 'You and your suntrap patios.'

On the way back I stopped outside the office. We were doing so well that we'd had it refurbished. In the window, each photo was mounted in a plastic cube, lit from within . . . glowing from the heart. CHARMING PERIOD HOUSE . . . DELIGHTFUL

GARDEN MAISONETTE. Beyond them I could see the shadowy room and my dark desk.

I thought of Marcus's words. Why was he such an expert, when he'd made such a mess of his own life?

I worked harder than ever the next couple of weeks. Houses move fast in July; people are restless.

I was restless too. I felt hot and cramped in the office. I spent a lot of time in my car, driving clients around and visiting new properties. Once I drove to Holland Park, just to see if I could pass down Nigel's street without my stomach churning. I stopped outside the house. The blinds were down; he had taken the family on holiday.

I knew that, of course. For the first time in four years, however, I didn't know where they had gone. Or even how long they would be away. I hadn't asked him.

For the first time I gave the house a long, honest look. I saw it for what it was: an imposing, terraced mansion with a pillared porch. There it stood, large and creamy. A family fortress.

I drove away. I had three appointments that afternoon, meeting prospective buyers at various empty properties.

Two of them passed without incident. At five o'clock only the last remained. It was not until then that I fished the third key from my bag, and found the piece of paper, where my secretary had noted down the person's name.

He was waiting outside in the street.

'It's you,' I said stupidly.

He grinned. 'It's me all right. I'm glad it's you.'

'What?'

'Not Prewitt or Little.'

'No. It's not them.'

We stood there by the front gate. Trying to collect my thoughts, I fiddled with the gate-latch. There was a moment's silence, then he pointed up at the house.

'Which floor's the flat?'

'The second. Didn't you know?'

'I just saw the board up, with your name on it. So I phoned.' He picked at the blisters on the fence. 'On impulse.'

I felt hot. I said: 'Thought you were looking in Barnes.'

'I looked. Everyone's married.'

'Even the actresses?'

'Even them.'

We stood there. He popped the blisters in the paint. He wore his tired-looking jacket.

'Didn't you go to work today?' I asked.

He shook his head. 'Went round looking at your boards.'

I moved towards the door. 'You won't like this flat.'

'Why?'

'Just being honest.'

We went upstairs. The flat was a new conversion. It had been flashed up with magnolia paint and woodchip wallpaper.

'Cowboy job,' I said.

'You are being unromantic today.'

We stood in the empty room.

'Vacant possession,' he murmured.

'Oh yes, it's that all right.'

He looked at me. Then he said: 'How are you, Celia?'

I gazed at the floorboards. 'All right.'

'How's things?'

I looked up at him. 'Oh, they're over.'

'Are they?'

I nodded. There was a silence.

Later we had a meal. Not at the bistro place; somewhere else. He said: 'I don't want that flat.'

I shook my head. 'No.'

'It's cheap and nasty.'

I nodded. 'Yes.'

'Are we both telling the truth now?'

'Yes.'

Afterwards we sat together in my Metro. The

car shook as lorries rumbled down the Cromwell Road.

I said: 'You feel so warm.'

'Oh yes,' he replied. 'I'm fully central-heated.'

CHARMING GARDEN-LEVEL FLAT. That's what he bought, and it means a basement, of course. It had a COUNTRY-STYLE garden which meant full of nettles but I've been seeing to those.

It is charming, too. I'm not just saying it. I've come to know every corner, over the past few weeks. It charms me.

· Some Day
My Prince Will Come ·

I was woken up by Tilly prising open my mouth. They'd had the school dentist yesterday, that was why. She was smug because they had found nothing wrong with her.

'Wider,' she said. Small ruthless fingers pushed back my lips, baring my gums. I was lying in bed and she was sitting on top of me. 'There's these bits here . . . yellowy bits . . . round the edges of your teeth.' Her calm eyes gazed into my mouth. 'It's called plaque,' she said. 'You should brush your teeth gooder.'

Beside me, Martin grunted. 'Seen the time?'

Tilly was now yanking down my lower jaw. 'Ooh, look at all your silver stuff.'

'Half past six,' said Martin, and went back to sleep.

'You've got lots of holes, didn't you,' she said.

Most of them, I thought, when I was pregnant with you. I lay, mute as a cow, under her gaze. She

215

was only five and already she made me feel inferior. She would say things like: 'You shouldn't smoke.' I hadn't the heart to reply: I didn't, till recently.

Tilly settled down to deeper inspection. I was going to say: go and look at Daddy's teeth. Then I thought: better not, he had a hard day yesterday, at the office. A long day ahead, too. It's Saturday, Working on the House Day. Every Saturday and every Sunday . . . weekends of the whirring Black & Decker, and fogs of dust, and muffled curses from the closed door behind which he toiled . . . of tripping over the plumbing pipes, and searching for one small sandal in the rubble, and keeping out of Daddy's way . . . So much of the time I spent protecting Martin from his children.

Tilly got bored and padded off in her nightie, sucking her thumb. From the back she suddenly looked terribly young. Outside I heard a thud: she had knocked down a roll of wallpaper.

'Hey!' Martin's head reared up. Where his tools were concerned his reaction was so sharp. I swear he could hear a chisel shifting in its box three rooms away. Funny how he could sleep through all the children's noises – the cries to be potted, the thud as *they* rolled over and fell out of bed.

However, this seemed a churlish waking thought, with a weekend ahead. I ticked myself off, running through the litany to make myself a more loving wife: Remember, Martin's slaving away just for us. Wasn't it me who wanted this house, such a lovely one right near the common, and we could never have afforded a done-up one in a street like this. And I bet he would rather spend the weekends playing football and watching the telly and drinking cans of lager . . . He would probably even prefer to spend them striding over the common with Tilly on his shoulders, like fathers did in Building Society advertisements. He had never done that. He said: there's so much to do.

Did your character change when you had children? Mine did. Trouble is, it's crept up on me so gradually and by now I simply can't remember what I was like before . . . What *we* were like. What did Martin and I do, those three years of long, child-free weekends in our flat? What does one do? Did we actually sit and talk, and read books unmolested, and wander off to the cinema on impulse, go anywhere on impulse, go to pubs . . . And dawdle in shops unembarrassed by clumsy infants and cold, shopgirl stares, and make love in the afternoons? That bit I do remember . . . I remember that.

Anyway, that Saturday I got up, and fed the children, and peeled off their Plasticine from Martin's hammer before he saw it . . . Really, compared to the rest of the week, weekends were such a strain

. . . And pulled a nail out of Tilly's plimsoll. She made such a fuss that I tried to shut her up by telling her the story about Androcles and the Lion, but I couldn't remember what had happened. Didn't Kirk Douglas play Androcles? By this time Tilly was wearing her schoolmistressy look. And Adam had just fallen down and was shrieking so loudly that Martin could hear him over the electric sander.

After lunch Martin went out. He had all these errands to do on Saturdays, like getting his hair cut and the car repaired, and things mended that I had forgotten to do during the week or that I had been too busy to fetch – he can't understand that I'm busy, when there's nothing to show for it. No floors re-laid, nothing like that. And he has to go to all those proper little shops with old men in overalls who take hours; he refuses to go to the big help-yourself places because he says they're soulless.

It's taking ages, our house. It's like one of those fairy stories where Mrs Hen won't give an egg until she's been given some straw, and Mr Horse won't give any straw until he's been given some sugar. You can't plumb in the bath until the skirting's fixed, and you can't fix the skirting until the dry rot's been done . . . I told this to Martin and he gazed at me and then he said: 'That reminds me. Forgot the Nitromors.'

It was two thirty and raining outside. Do you ever have those moments of dulled panic: what on earth can one possibly do with the children until bedtime? The afternoon stretched ahead; Adam was staggering around, scattering wood shavings. Then I looked in the local paper and saw that *Snow White* was on.

So I wrote a note to Martin and heaved out the double buggy and spent 23½ minutes searching for their gumboots and gloves . . . I actually went to college once, would you believe, and I can still add up . . . 12½ minutes to find my bag, and the teddy that Adam has to suck.

I pushed the children along the street – at least, Adam sat in the buggy (he's just three) and Tilly walked beside me because she only sits in the buggy when she's sure not to meet any of her friends.

'Does Snow White wear a beautiful pink dress?' she asked. 'With frillies?' She's obsessed with pink.

'Can't remember,' I said. 'I was your age when I saw it. I loved it more than any film I've ever seen.'

'Snow White gets deaded,' said Adam.

'She doesn't!' I cried. 'She's only asleep.'

'Deaded in a box. Seen the picture.'

'She isn't! She's just sleeping. And do you know how she wakes?'

'Got worms in her.'

'Shut up. She wakes up when the Prince comes along,' I said.

'Why?'

'He kisses her.'

When did Martin last kiss me? Properly. Or when, indeed, did I last kiss him?

The Prince just touches her forehead, or is it her lips? Just a peck, really. Just like when Martin comes home from the office.

No, not like that at all.

'Mummy! I said what happens after that?' Tilly's addressing-the-retarded voice. 'Does she get a baby? Does she get married?'

'Oh yes, they marry all right. He takes her off to his castle in the sunset, on the back of his big white horse.'

We arrived at the cinema; a peeling brick cliff, its neon lights glaring over the grey street. How could such buildings house such impossible dreams?

Inside I saw him. I saw him straight away; the place was half-empty. But I would have spotted him, I bet, in a crowd of a thousand. He was flung back in his seat, in that abandoned way he had, with his hair sticking up like it always had. He had never taken care of himself. The lights were still up; if I'd dared I'd have looked longer.

I had sat next to him in fifty cinema seats . . .
Him beside me, flung back in that restless, tense
way, never settled . . . his arm lying along the back
of the seat. But now his arms were flung each side
of his children.

'Let's go here!' Tilly demanded.

I pulled her away.

'Mummy! We can see over the edge!'

'Come on. This way.'

'Don't be silly! There's all these seats.'

'Silly bum-bum,' said Adam.

I dragged the buggy further away.

'Wanna sit here,' cried Adam.

'Ssh!'

I sat them down at last, pulling off their anoraks
and trying to shove the buggy under the seat. The
cinema darkened.

'Gimme the popcorn!' said Adam.

I rummaged in my carrier-bag. While I did it,
I stole another look. A red point glowed . . . She
hadn't stopped him smoking, then.

'You said half!' Tilly hissed.

'Have a handful each.'

'S'not fair! He's –'

'Ssh! It's starting.'

Snow White was washing the steps, scrubbing
and singing, the birds cheeping. I thought: forgot
the Daz, and now I've missed the shops.

'When's the Prince coming?' hissed Tilly, her mouth full of popcorn.

'Hang on,' I replied. 'Don't be impatient.'

'Will he come on his horse?'

'Of course.'

He'd had a motorbike, an old Triumph. I'd sat behind him, gripping him with my arms, my face pressed against the leather. Ah, the ache, that his skin was hidden . . . The physical pain, that I couldn't get my hands on him. I wanted him all the time. Where did we go? Transport cafés at four in the morning. The glare of the light, the suddenness of all those strangers, after we had been alone for so long . . . He'd take off his gloves and hold my hand; I stroked his hard fingernails, one by one, and then the wider nail of his thumb.

Afterwards, driving oh too fast – he had a death wish all right – driving just for the heck of it . . . Then back to my digs, lying naked on the twisted sheets, the sun glowing through the curtains and the children down in the street whooping on their way to school – they seemed a hundred miles away . . . And me missing my lectures.

I wish you had met him. You'd probably think he was wildly unsuitable, far too neurotic. My parents did. They were terrified that I would marry him. And I didn't, did I?

I wonder if you'd have thought him beautiful. I

wondered if he still was. It was too dark to see. All I'd heard was that he had married a social worker and had two children. She was called Joyce. I'd pictured somebody with a political conscience and thick ankles, who would care for him and see that he ate. Well, that's how I liked to picture her. Today she must be staying home, making flans for the freezer. Did he write her poetry, like he had written for me? Did anybody, once they got married? Joyce . . . With a name like that, she must be overweight.

'*Mirror mirror on the wall, who's the fairest one of all?*'

The Dark Queen was up on the screen, with her bitter, beautiful face. The light flared on her.

A hand gripped mine. 'She's horrid!' said Tilly.

'She's jealous,' I whispered.

'I hate her.'

'Ssh.'

Where did he live? It must be around here. On the other hand, on a wet Saturday afternoon he might have crossed London to see *Snow White*.

I would follow him home. I'd find out where he lived and press my nose against the window and gaze into his life, his lamplit family life all unknown to me, where I was not needed . . .

'Ugh!' The hand squeezed. 'She's turning into a witch!'

'Look at her horrid nose!'

'Isn't she ugly.'

'I don't like her!'

Tilly said in her posh voice: 'It's because she's got ugly thoughts.'

She took away her hand and sat there primly. She was wearing her kilt that she'd chosen herself, and her awful orange plastic necklace, and her I'VE SEEN WINDSOR SAFARI PARK badge.

Snow White was in the forest now; it was blacker than Windsor Park and the trees were swaying and moaning, warning her of danger. I thought that Tilly would be frightened here but she didn't show it. I had a sudden desire to grip my growing, wayward girl, so cool and so young. I wanted to grip her and protect her from what lay ahead. But she disliked shows of emotion.

Snow White had arrived at the dwarfs' cottage and, little housewife that she was, she was clearing up, dusting, polishing, a song on her lips (well, she had about twenty squirrels and rabbits to help). I looked round. He was getting up.

I felt panic. But he was only carrying out one of his children, down the aisle. They must be going to the lavatory. He passed quite close, gripping the child. He was wearing a pale pullover and he held the child so tenderly. Ten years later and he looked just the same, no fatter. I thought how easily that child could have been ours. It could have been us sitting there, and no Tilly. No Adam. Or a different Tilly . . .

'Mummy, you're hurting!'

I had been squeezing her hand, so I took mine away. But then she groped for it – both of them did – because the witch was knocking on the door of the cottage.

I feared for his remaining child, left alone. But I stopped myself. It wasn't my child to worry about. Besides, there he was, his hair haloed by the screen, bowed so he wouldn't block the view of this terrifying, powerful film.

Snow White let in the witch. As she took the apple, the audience sat absolutely still. All those children – not a sweetpaper rustled. Nothing.

When she bit the apple, Tilly hid her face. My cool, superior Tilly. I pressed my hand against her eyes.

'It's all right,' I whispered.

'I want to go.'

'It's all right,' I said desperately. 'I told you – the Prince will come.'

He came, of course, as you knew he would. He rode up on his muscular white horse. Tilly took away her hand; she sat there, calm as ever. She knew it would turn out all right.

The Prince knelt down to kiss Snow White. And then she was in his arms and he was lifting her

on to the back of his horse. Not a motorbike –
a stallion with a thick curved neck, and the sun
cast long shadows between the trees as they rode
off, and ahead lay the castle, radiant.

Businesslike, Tilly was rummaging in the bottom
of the popcorn bag. I sat limp; I felt her busy
concentration. She knew the Prince would come,
she believed it. Every girl must believe it, because
wouldn't life be insupportable if they didn't?

'Come on.' She was standing up.

Every girl . . . Every boy too. All those young,
believing children.

'Where's your hanky?' I muttered.

She had this hideous little diamanté handbag that
Aunt Nelly had given her; she carried it everywhere.
I took the hanky and blew my nose. The lights
came on.

'Don't be soppy,' she said. 'It's only a story.'

I saw him ahead of us in the foyer. He had sunk
down in front of his child and was zipping up
its anorak. He was speaking but I couldn't hear
the words.

Outside it was dark, and still raining: a soft
November drizzle. I saw him quite clearly standing
at the bus stop on the other side of the road. His
children looked younger than mine.

I wanted to follow him. I couldn't face meeting

him but I wanted to see where he lived. I wanted to set him into a house and give him a locality. I would be able to dream about him better then. All these years he had just been the same set of memories, stale and repeated; his present life was a vacuum. I hungered even for the name of his street.

'I'm wet!'

'Wanna Slush Puppy!'

'I want to go home.'

I wonder if you would have followed him.

I didn't. It was cold out there, and dark, and fumey as people revved up their cars. The warmth of the cinema, the dreams, they had vanished like that castle into the raw air of this South London road. Really, what was the good? Besides, the person I was seeking belonged to somebody who no longer existed.

They both sat in the buggy, they were so sleepy. I gazed down at their two anorak hoods, lolling, brown in the sodium light. Some day, I thought, will your Prince come? If you get lost in the dark wood, as you will, and I can't always be there to protect you . . . If you get lost, will somebody find you? Will you be happy?

Twenty minutes later I was walking up our street. The cardboard eye of our bedroom looked at me blankly. It said: *shouldn't have gone, should you?*

Our car was outside and the house lights were on. Martin must be home. The rain had stopped but I wiped my face on my sleeve. Besides, he would just think my face was wet from the rain. If, that is, he ever noticed anything about me.

I went into the house, with its naked lightbulb hanging down. The light shone on a lot of planks, propped against the wall; they made a forest of the hallway. He had been to the timber merchant.

Adam stirred and started to whine. Tilly climbed out of the pushchair and they went into the living-room. A burst of canned laughter; they had switched on the TV.

Martin didn't come out of the kitchen. No buzzing drill. I hesitated. Could he feel my thoughts? In the sitting-room the advertisements came on; I heard the jingle for the Midland Bank. The children call it the Middling Bank.

Then I thought: he's made me a surprise.

I stood still, the realization filling me, through my limbs, like warm liquid.

You know how, just when the children are driving you insane, when you can't stand another minute . . . You know how, suddenly, they do something terribly touching? Like drawing you a card with I LOVE MUM on it or trying, disastrously, to do the washing up?

Martin had made the supper. Hopelessly, because

228

he couldn't cook. But he had cleared the table, and bought a bottle of wine and lots of pricey things from the deli. He had realized how I'd been feeling lately.

I opened the door. But this wasn't a story. Life is not that neat, is it? No fairy tale.

There sat Martin, with a can of beer in front of him and the lunch plates still piled in the sink. Packets were heaped on the table: not exotic cheeses but three-point plugs and boxes of nails.

'Hello.' He looked up. 'Didn't hear you come in.'

'Exhausted?'

He nodded. Fiction is shapely. A story billows out like a sheet, then comes the final knot. *The End*. Reared up against the suffused, pink sky there stands a castle, lit from within. The end.

A silence as he poured the lager into his glass. The froth filled up; we both watched it. He said: 'The end is in sight. I think I can finally say I've finished this bloody kitchen.'

Also by Deborah Moggach and available in paperback

Seesaw

Take an ordinary, well-off family like the Prices. Watch what happens when one Sunday seventeen-year-old Hannah disappears without a trace. See how the family rallies when a ransom note demands half a million pounds for Hannah's safe return.

But it's when Hannah comes home that the story really begins.

Now observe what happens to a family when they lose their house, their status, all their wealth. Note how they disintegrate under the pressures of guilt and poverty and are forced to confront their true selves.

And finally, wait to hear all about Hannah, who has the most shocking surprise in store of all.

'Provocative, enthralling, bang-up-to-the-minute . . . truly, Moggach gets better and better' Val Hennessy, *Daily Mail*

'A delight to read' *Daily Telegraph*

Close Relations

The three Hammond sisters have each chosen their own paths. Louise leads a seemingly perfect existence in Beaconsfield with her venture-capitalist husband, messy teenage children and Smallbone kitchen. Prudence, who has successfully forged a career in publishing, is having a fruitless affair with her married boss. And Maddy, always the square peg in the round hole, has just met and fallen in love with a lesbian gardener.

When their father, Gordon, has a heart attack and ten runs away to live in Brixton with a young black nurse, Dorothy – his wife – is released like a loose cannon into her daughters' lives.

As passions run high, relationships break up and dramatic developments look set to change them all for ever. For better or for worse.

'A compassionate family comedy . . . Moggach writes of the calamity of love and the devastation of divorce. A novel of comic appeal and topical with' *Times Literary Supplement*

'Moggach is a skilful narrator, deftly weaving together the threads of each family member's life, creating an instantly recognisable world' *Daily Telegraph*

Porky

At school they called her Porky on account of the pigs her family kept outside the bungalow near Heathrow. But she felt no different – not until she realised she was losing her innocence in a way that none of her friends could possibly imagine. Only a child robbed of her childhood can know too late what it means to be loved too little and loved too much . . .

'Deborah Moggach conveys with chilling skill the process by which a fundamentally bright, decent child becomes infested by corruption' *Spectator*

'Illuminates with great compassion how love can so easily go off the rails' *Daily Mail*

'At once eerily exuberant and bleak, this is a compassionate, tough book' *Observer*

'Extraordinarily skilful' Anita Brookner

Driving in the Dark

Desmond never did have much luck with women – except in getting them through their driving tests. Now a coach driver, he is at the most crucial crossroads of his life. His wife has thrown him out. The crisis serves only to deepen his despair over another failed liaison – until he elects to steer his coach on a spectacularly reckless quest for the son he has never seen.

'Disturbing and witty . . . a deftly-described odyssey that places the battle of the sexes in a new arena' *Sunday Times*

'Moggach, for the purposes of this book, has turned herself into a bloke. His monologue throughout strikes me as totally authentic, but not only does Moggach get his lingo right, she thinks through his head, dramatizing his confusion, decency, wit, pain and determination. This is not just ventriloquism, but empathy so complete as to be phenomenal' *Irish Times*

'At once acutely funny and sad . . . a woman's protest at the inequality thrust on men by the worst excesses of the woman's movement' *Mail on Sunday*

'Poignant and funny . . . Deborah Moggach is brilliant at capturing just the right voice for her characters' *Cosmopolitan*

A Selected List of Fiction Available from Mandarin and Arrow

ALL BOOKS ARE AVAILABLE THROUGH MAIL ORDER OR FROM YOUR LOCAL BOOKSHOP AND NEWSAGENT.

PLEASE SEND CHEQUE/EUROCHEQUE/POSTAL ORDER (STERLING ONLY) ACCESS, VISA, DINERS CARD, SWITCH, AMEX OR MASTERCARD.

EXPIRY DATE .... SIGNATURE ....

PLEASE ALLOW 75 PENCE PER BOOK FOR POST AND PACKING U.K.

OVERSEAS CUSTOMERS PLEASE ALLOW £1.00 PER COPY FOR POST AND PACKING.

ALL ORDERS TO:

ARROW BOOKS, BOOKS BY POST, TBS LIMITED, THE BOOK SERVICE, COLCHESTER ROAD, FRATING GREEN, COLCHESTER, ESSEX CO7 7DW.

NAME ....

ADDRESS ....

....

Please allow 28 days for delivery. Please tick box if you do not wish to receive any additional information ☐

Prices and availability subject to change without notice.